W9-BXM-063

JUL - - 2013

KEEPER OF THE BRIDE

KEEPER OF THE BRIDE

Tess Gerritsen

This first world hardcover edition published 2013
in Great Britain and in the USA by
SEVERN HOUSE PUBLISHERS LTD of
19 Cedar Road, Sutton, Surrey, England, SM2 5DA,
by arrangement with Harlequin Books.
First published 1996 in the USA in mass market format only.

British Library Cataloguing in Publication Data

Gerritsen, Tess.
  Keeper of the bride.
  1. Romantic suspense novels.
  I. Title
  813.6-dc23

  ISBN-13: 978-0-7278-8122-9   (cased)

All Severn House titles are printed on acid-free paper.

Severn House Publishers support The Forest Stewardship Council [FSC],
the leading international forest certification organisation. All our titles that
are printed on Greenpeace-approved FSC-certified paper carry the FSC logo.

MIX
Paper from
responsible sources
FSC
www.fsc.org   FSC® C018575

Printed and bound in Great Britain by
MPG Books Ltd., Bodmin, Cornwall.

JUL - 1 2013

One

The wedding was off. Cancelled. Canned. Kaput.

Nina Cormier sat staring at herself in the church dressing room mirror and wondered why she couldn't seem to cry. She knew the pain was there, deep and terrible beneath the numbness, but she didn't feel it. Not yet. She could only sit dry-eyed, staring at her reflection. The picture-perfect image of a bride. Her veil floated in gossamer wisps about her face. The bodice of her ivory satin dress, embroidered with seed pearls, hung fetchingly off-shoulder. Her long black hair was gathered into a soft chignon. Everyone who'd seen her that morning in the dressing room—her mother, her sister, Wendy, her stepmother, Daniella—had declared her a beautiful bride.

And she *would* have been. Had the groom bothered to show up.

He didn't even have the courage to break the news to her in person. After six months of planning and dreaming, she'd received his note just twenty minutes before the ceremony. Via the best man, no less.

Nina,

I need time to think about this. I'm sorry, I really am. I'm leaving town for a few days. I'll call you.

Robert

She forced herself to read the note again.

I need time…. I need time….

How much time does a man need? she wondered.

A year ago, she'd moved in with Dr. Robert Bledsoe. It's the only way to know if we're compatible, he'd told her. Marriage was such a major commitment, a permanent commitment, and he didn't want to make a mistake. At 41, Robert had known his share of disastrous relationships. He was determined not to make any more mistakes. He wanted to be sure that Nina was the one he'd been waiting for all his life.

She'd been certain Robert was the man *she'd* been waiting for. So certain that, on the very day he'd suggested they live together, she'd gone straight home and packed her bags….

"Nina? Nina, open the door!" It was her sister, Wendy, rattling the knob. "Please let me in."

Nina dropped her head in her hands. "I don't want to see anyone right now."

"You need to be with someone."

"I just want to be alone."

"Look, the guests have all gone home. The church is empty. It's just me out here."

"I don't want to talk to anyone. Just go home, will you? Please, just go."

There was a long silence outside the door. Then Wendy said, "If I leave now, how're you going to get home? You'll need a ride."

"Then I'll call a cab. Or Reverend Sullivan can drive me.
I need some time to think."

"You're sure you don't want to talk?"

"I'm sure. I'll call you later, okay?"

"If that's what you really want." Wendy paused, then
added, with a note of venom that penetrated even through
the oak door, "Robert's a jerk, you know. I might as well
tell you. I've always thought he was."

Nina didn't answer. She sat at the dressing table, her
head in her hands, wanting to cry, but unable to squeeze
out a single tear. She heard Wendy's footsteps fade away,
then heard only the silence of the empty church. Still no
tears would come. She couldn't think about Robert right
now. Instead, her mind seemed to focus stubbornly on the
practical aspects of a cancelled wedding. The catered reception and all that uneaten food. The gifts she had to
return. The nonrefundable airline tickets to St. John Island.
Maybe she should go on that honeymoon anyway and
forget Dr. Robert Bledsoe. She'd go by herself, just her and
her bikini. Out of this whole heartbreaking affair, at least
she'd come out with a tan.

Slowly she raised her head and once again looked at her
reflection in the mirror. Not such a beautiful bride after all,
she thought. Her lipstick was smeared and her chignon was
coming apart. She was turning into a wreck.

With sudden rage she reached up and yanked off the veil.
Hairpins flew in every direction, releasing a rebellious
tumble of black hair. To hell with the veil; she tossed it in
the trash can. She snatched up her bouquet of white lilies and
pink sweetheart roses and slam-dunked it into the trash can
as well. That felt good. Her anger was like some new and
potent fuel flooding her veins. It propelled her to her feet.

She walked out of the church dressing room, the train of her gown dragging behind her, and entered the nave.

The pews were deserted. Garlands of white carnations draped the aisles, and the altar was adorned with airy sprays of pink roses and baby's breath. The stage had been beautifully set for a wedding that would never take place. But the lovely results of the florist's hard work was scarcely noticed by Nina as she strode past the altar and started up the aisle. Her attention was focused straight ahead on the front door. On escape. Even the concerned voice of Reverend Sullivan calling to her didn't slow her down. She walked past all the floral reminders of the day's fiasco and pushed through the double doors.

There, on the church steps, she halted. The July sunshine glared in her eyes, and she was suddenly, painfully aware of how conspicuous she must be, a lone woman in a wedding gown, trying to wave down a taxi. Only then, as she stood trapped in the brightness of afternoon, did she feel the first sting of tears.

Oh, no. Lord, no. She was going to break down and cry right here on the steps. In full view of every damn car driving past on Forest Avenue.

"Nina? Nina, dear."

She turned. Reverend Sullivan was standing on the step above her, a look of worry on his kind face.

"Is there anything I can do? Anything at all?" he asked. "If you'd like, we could go inside and talk."

Miserably she shook her head. "I want to get away from here. Please, I just want to get away."

"Of course. Of course." Gently, he took her arm. "I'll drive you home."

Reverend Sullivan led her down the steps and around

the side of the building, to the staff parking lot. She gathered up her train, which by now was soiled from all that dragging, and climbed into his car. There she sat with all the satin piled high on her lap.

Reverend Sullivan slid in behind the wheel. The heat was stifling inside the car, but he didn't start the engine. Instead they sat for a moment in awkward silence.

"I know it's hard to understand what possible purpose the Lord may have for all this," he said quietly. "But surely there's a reason, Nina. It may not be apparent to you at the moment. In fact, it may seem to you that the Lord has turned His back."

"Robert's the one who turned his back," she said. Sniffling, she snatched up a clean corner of her train and wiped her face. "Turned his back and ran like hell."

"Ambivalence is common for bridegrooms. I'm sure Dr. Bledsoe felt this was a big step for him—"

"A big step for *him?* I suppose marriage is just a stroll in the park for me?"

"No, no, you misunderstand me."

"Oh, please." She gave a muffled sob. "Just take me home."

Shaking his head, he put the key in the ignition. "I only wanted to explain to you, dear, in my own clumsy way, that this isn't the end of the world. It's the nature of life. Fate is always throwing surprises at us, Nina. Crises we never expect. Things that seem to pop right out of the blue."

A deafening boom suddenly shook the church building. The explosion shattered the stained glass windows, and a hail of multicolored glass shards flew across the parking lot. Torn hymn books and fragments of church pews tumbled onto the blacktop.

As the white smoke slowly cleared, Nina saw a dusting of flower petals drift gently down from the sky and settle on the windshield right in front of Reverend Sullivan's shocked eyes.

"Right out of the blue," she murmured. "You couldn't have said it better."

"YOU TWO, WITHOUT A DOUBT, are the biggest screwups of the year."

Portland police detective Sam Navarro, sitting directly across the table from the obviously upset Norm Liddell, didn't bat an eyelash. There were five of them sitting in the station conference room, and Sam wasn't about to give this prima donna D.A. the satisfaction of watching him flinch in public. Nor was Sam going to refute the charges, because they *had* screwed up. He and Gillis had screwed up big time, and now a cop was dead. An idiot cop, but a cop all the same. One of their own.

"In our defense," spoke up Sam's partner, Gordon Gillis, "we never gave Marty Pickett permission to approach the site. We had no idea he'd crossed the police line—"

"You were in charge of the bomb scene," said Liddell. "That makes you responsible."

"Now, wait a minute," said Gillis. "Officer Pickett has to bear some of the blame."

"Pickett was just a rookie."

"He should've been following procedure. If he'd—"

"Shut up, Gillis," said Sam.

Gillis looked at his partner. "Sam, I'm only trying to defend our position."

"Won't do us a damn bit of good. Since we're obviously the designated fall guys." Sam leaned back in his chair and eyed Liddell across the conference table. "What do you want, Mr. D.A.? A public flogging? Our resignations?"

"No one's asking for your resignations," cut in Chief Abe Coopersmith. "And this discussion is getting us nowhere."

"*Some* disciplinary action is called for," said Liddell. "We have a dead police officer—"

"Don't you think I know that?" snapped Coopersmith. "*I'm* the one who had to answer to the widow. Not to mention all those bloodsucking reporters. Don't give me this *us* and *we* crap, Mr. D.A. It was one of *ours* who fell. A cop. *Not* a lawyer."

Sam looked in surprise at his chief. This was a new experience, having Coopersmith on his side. The Abe Coopersmith he knew was a man of few words, few of them complimentary. It was because Liddell was rubbing them all the wrong way. When under fire, cops always stuck together.

"Let's get back to the business at hand, okay?" said Coopersmith. "We have a bomber in town. And our first fatality. What do we know so far?" He looked at Sam, who was head of the newly re-formed Bomb Task Force. "Navarro?"

"Not a hell of a lot," admitted Sam. He opened a file folder and took out a sheaf of papers. He distributed copies to the other four men around the table—Liddell, Chief Coopersmith, Gillis, and Ernie Takeda, the explosives expert from the Maine State Crime Lab. "The first blast occurred around 2:15 a.m. The second blast around 2:30 a.m. It was the second one that pretty much levelled the R. S. Hancock warehouse. It also caused minor damage to two adjoining buildings. The night watchman was the one who found the first device. He noticed signs of breaking and entering, so he searched the building. The bomb was left on a desk in one of the offices. He put in the call at 1:30 a.m.

Gillis got there around 1:50, I was there at 2:00 a.m. We had the blast area cordoned off and the top-vent container truck had just arrived when the first one went off. Then, fifteen minutes later—before we could search the building—the second device exploded. Killing Officer Pickett." Sam glanced at Liddell, but this time the D.A. chose to keep his mouth shut. "The dynamite was Dupont label."

There was a brief silence in the room. Then Cooper-smith said, "Not the same Dupont lot number as those two bombs last year?"

"It's very likely," said Sam. "Since that missing lot number's the only reported large dynamite theft we've had up here in years."

"But the Spectre bombings were solved a year ago," said Liddell. "And we know Vincent Spectre's dead. So who's making *these* bombs?"

"We may be dealing with a Spectre apprentice. Some-one who not only picked up the master's technique, but also has access to the master's dynamite supply. Which, I point out, we never located."

"You haven't confirmed the dynamite's from the same stolen lot number," said Liddell. "Maybe this has no con-nection at all with the Spectre bombings."

"I'm afraid we have other evidence," said Sam. "And you're not going to like it." He glanced at Ernie Takeda. "Go ahead, Ernie."

Takeda, never comfortable with public speaking, kept his gaze focused on the lab report in front of him. "Based on materials we gathered at the site," he said, "we can make a preliminary guess as to the makeup of the device. We believe the electrical action fuse was set off by an elec-tronic delay circuit. This in turn ignited the dynamite via

Prima detonating cord. The sticks were bundled together with two-inch-wide green electrical tape." Takeda cleared his throat and finally looked up. "It's the identical delay circuit that the late Vincent Spectre used in his bombings last year."

Liddell looked at Sam. "The same circuitry, the same dynamite lot? What the hell's going on?"

"Obviously," said Gillis, "Vincent Spectre passed on a few of his skills before he died. Now we've got a second generation bomber on our hands."

"What we still have to piece together," said Sam, "is the psychological profile of this newcomer. Spectre's bombings were coldbloodedly financial. He was hired to do the jobs and he did them, *bam, bam, bam.* Efficient. Effective. This new bomber has to set a pattern."

"What you're saying," said Liddell, "is that you expect him to hit again."

Sam nodded wearily. "Unfortunately, that's exactly what I'm saying."

There was a knock on the door. A patrolwoman stuck her head into the conference room. "Excuse me, but there's a call for Navarro and Gillis."

"I'll take it," said Gillis. He rose heavily to his feet and went to the conference wall phone.

Liddell was still focused on Sam. "So this is all that Portland's finest can come up with? We wait for *another* bombing so that we can establish a *pattern?* And then maybe, just *maybe,* we'll have an idea of what the hell we're doing?"

"A bombing, Mr. Liddell," said Sam calmly, "is an act of cowardice. It's violence in the absence of the perpetrator. I repeat the word—*absence.* We have no ID, no fingerprints, no witnesses to the planting, no—"

"Chief," cut in Gillis. He hung up the phone. "They've just reported another one."

"What?" said Coopersmith.

Sam had already shot to his feet and was moving for the door.

"What was it this time?" called Liddell. "Another warehouse?"

"No," said Gillis. "A church."

THE COPS ALREADY had the area cordoned off by the time Sam and Gillis arrived at the Good Shepherd Church. A crowd was gathered up and down the street. Three patrol cars, two fire trucks and an ambulance were parked haphazardly along Forest Avenue. The bomb disposal truck and its boiler-shaped carrier in the flatbed stood idly near the church's front entrance—or what was left of the front entrance. The door had been blown clear off its hinges and had come to rest at the bottom of the front steps. Broken glass was everywhere. The wind scattered torn pages of hymn books like dead leaves along the sidewalk. Gillis swore. "This was a big one."

As they approached the police line, the officer in charge turned to them with a look of relief. "Navarro! Glad you could make it to the party."

"Any casualties?" asked Sam.

"None, as far as we know. The church was unoccupied at the time. Pure luck. There was a wedding scheduled for two, but it was cancelled at the last minute."

"Whose wedding?"

"Some doctor's. The bride's sitting over there in the patrol car. She and the minister witnessed the blast from the parking lot."

"I'll talk to her later," said Sam. "Don't let her leave. Or the minister, either. I'm going to check the building for a second device."

"Better you than me."

Sam donned body armor, made of overlapping steel plates encased in nylon. He also carried a protective mask, to be worn in case a second bomb was identified. A bomb tech, similarly garbed, stood by the front door awaiting orders to enter the building. Gillis would wait outside near the truck; his role this time around was to fetch tools and get the bomb carrier ready.

"Okay," Sam said to the technician. "Let's go."

They stepped through the gaping front entrance.

The first thing Sam noticed was the smell—strong and faintly sweet. Dynamite, he thought. He recognized the odor of its aftermath. The force of the blast had caused the pews at the rear to topple backward. At the front, near the altar, the pews had been reduced to splinters. All the stained glass panels were broken, and where the windows faced south, hazy sunlight shone in through the empty frames.

Without a word between them, Sam and the tech automatically split up and moved along opposite sides of the nave. The site would be more thoroughly searched later; this time around, their focus was only on locating any second bombs. The death of Marty Pickett still weighed heavily on Sam's conscience, and he wasn't about to let any other officers enter this building until he had cleared it.

Moving in parallel, the two men paced the nave, their eyes alert for anything resembling an explosive device. All the debris made it a slow search. As they moved forward, the damage visibly worsened, and the odor of exploded

dynamite grew stronger. Getting closer, he thought. The
bomb was planted somewhere around here....

In front of the altar, at a spot where the first row of pews
would have stood, they found the crater. It was about three
feet across and shallow; the blast had ripped through the
carpet and pad, but had barely chipped the concrete slab
below. A shallow crater was characteristic of a low-
velocity blast—again, compatible with dynamite.

They would take a closer look at it later. They continued their search. They finished with the nave and pro-
gressed to the hallways, the dressing rooms, the restrooms.
No bombs. They went into the annex and surveyed the
church offices, the meeting rooms, the Sunday school
classroom. No bombs. They exited through a rear door and
searched the entire outside wall. No bombs.

Satisfied at last, Sam returned to the police line,
where Gillis was waiting. There he took off the body
armor. "Building's clean," Sam said. "We got the searchers assembled?"

Gillis gestured to the six men waiting near the bomb
carrier truck. There were two patrolmen and four crime lab
techs, each one clutching empty evidence bags. "They're
just waiting for the word."

"Let's get the photographer in there first, then send the
team in. The crater's up front, around the first row of pews
on the right."

"Dynamite?"

Sam nodded. "If I can trust my nose." He turned and
eyed the crowd of gawkers. "I'm going to talk to the witnesses. Where's the minister?"

"They just took him off to the ER. Chest pains. All
that stress."

Sam gave an exasperated sigh. "Did anyone talk to him?"

"Patrolman did. We have his statement."

"Okay," said Sam. "I guess that leaves me with the bride."

"She's still waiting in the patrol car. Her name's Nina Cormier."

"Cormier. Gotcha." Sam ducked under the yellow police line and worked his way through the gathering of onlookers. Scanning the official vehicles, he spotted a silhouette in the front passenger seat of one of the cars. The woman didn't move as he approached; she was staring straight ahead like some wedding store mannequin. He leaned forward and tapped on the window.

The woman turned. Wide dark eyes stared at him through the glass. Despite the smudged mascara, the softly rounded feminine face was undeniably pretty. Sam motioned to her to roll down the window. She complied.

"Miss Cormier? I'm Detective Sam Navarro, Portland police."

"I want to go home," she said. "I've talked to so many cops already. Please, can't I just go home?"

"First I have to ask you a few questions."

"A few?"

"All right," he admitted. "It's more like a lot of questions."

She gave a sigh. Only then did he see the weariness in her face. "If I answer all your questions, Detective," she said, "will you let me go home?"

"I promise."

"Do you keep your promises?"

He nodded soberly. "Always."

She looked down at her hands, clasped in her lap. "Right," she muttered. "Men and their promises."

"Excuse me?"

"Oh, never mind."

He circled around the car, opened the door, and slid in behind the wheel. The woman next to him said nothing; she just sat there in resigned silence. She seemed almost swallowed up by those frothy layers of white satin. Her hairdo was coming undone and silky strands of black hair hung loose about her shoulders. Not at all the happy picture of a bride, he thought. She seemed stunned, and very much alone.

Where the hell was the groom?

Stifling an instinctive rush of sympathy, he reached for his notebook and flipped it open to a blank page. "Can I have your full name and address?"

The answer came out in a bare whisper. "Nina Margaret Cormier, 318 Ocean View Drive."

He wrote it down. Then he looked at her. She was still staring straight down at her lap. Not at him. "Okay, Miss Cormier," he said. "Why don't you tell me exactly what happened?"

SHE WANTED TO GO HOME. She had been sitting in this patrol car for an hour and a half now, had talked to three different cops, had answered all their questions. Her wedding was a shambles, she'd barely escaped with her life, and those people out there on the street kept staring at her as though she were some sort of sideshow freak.

And this man, this cop with all the warmth of a codfish, expected her to go through it again?

"Miss Cormier," he sighed. "The sooner we get this over with, the sooner you can leave. What, exactly, happened?"

"It blew up," she said. "Can I go home?"

"What do you mean by blew up?"

"There was a loud boom. Lots of smoke and broken windows. I'd say it was your typical exploding building."

"You mentioned smoke. What color was the smoke?"

"What?"

"Was it black? White?"

"Does it matter?"

"Just answer the question, please."

She gave an exasperated sigh. "It was white, I think."

"You think?"

"All right. I'm sure." She turned to look at him. For the first time she really focused on his face. If he'd been smiling, if there'd been even a trace of warmth, it would have been a pleasant enough face to look at. He was in his late thirties. He had dark brown hair that was about two weeks overdue for a trim. His face was thin, his teeth were perfect, and his deep set green eyes had the penetrating gaze one expected of a romantic lead movie cop. Only this was no movie cop. This was an honest-to-goodness cop with a badge, and he wasn't in the least bit charming. He was studying her with a completely detached air, as though sizing up her reliability as a witness.

She gazed back at him, thinking, *Here I am, the rejected bride. He's probably wondering what's wrong with me. What terrible flaws I possess that led to my being stood up at the altar.*

She buried her fists in the white satin mounded on her lap. "I'm sure the smoke was white," she said tightly. "For whatever difference that makes."

"It makes a difference. It indicates a relative absence of carbon."

"Oh. I see." Whatever that told him.

"Were there any flames?"

"No. No flames."

"Did you smell anything?"

"You mean like gas?"

"Anything at all?"

She frowned. "Not that I remember. But I was outside the building."

"Where, exactly?"

"Reverend Sullivan and I were sitting in his car. In the parking lot around the side. So I wouldn't have smelled the gas. Anyway, natural gas is odorless. Isn't it?"

"It can be difficult to detect."

"So it doesn't mean anything. That I didn't smell it."

"Did you see anyone near the building prior to the explosion?"

"There was Reverend Sullivan. And some of my family. But they all left earlier."

"What about strangers? Anyone you don't know?"

"No one was inside when it happened."

"I'm referring to the time *prior* to the explosion, Miss Cormier."

"Prior?"

"Did you see anyone who shouldn't have been there?"

She stared at him. He gazed back at her, green eyes absolutely steady. "You mean—are you thinking—"

He didn't say anything.

"It wasn't a gas leak?" she said softly.

"No," he said. "It was a bomb."

She sank back, her breath escaping in a single shocked rush. Not an accident, she thought. Not an accident at all....

"Miss Cormier?"

Wordlessly she looked at him. Something about the way he was watching her, that flat, emotionless gaze of his, made her frightened.

"I'm sorry to have to ask you this next question," he said. "But you understand, it's something I have to pursue."

She swallowed. "What...what question?"

"Do you know of anyone who might want you dead?"

Two

"This is crazy," she said. "This is absolutely nuts."

"I have to explore the possibility."

"*What* possibility? That the bomb was meant for *me?*"

"Your wedding was scheduled for two o'clock. The bomb went off at 2:40. It exploded near the front row of pews. Near the altar. There's no doubt in my mind, judging by the obvious force of the blast, that you and your entire wedding party would have been killed. Or, at the very least, seriously maimed. This *is* a bomb we're talking about, Miss Cormier. Not a gas leak. Not an accident. A bomb. It was meant to kill someone. What I have to find out is, who was the target?"

She didn't answer. The possibilities were too horrible to even contemplate.

"Who was in your wedding party?" he asked.

She swallowed. "There was…there was…"

"You and Reverend Sullivan. Who else?"

"Robert—my fiancé. And my sister, Wendy. And Jeremy Wall, the best man.…"

"Anyone else?"

"My father was going to give me away. And there was a flower girl and a ring bearer..."

"I'm only interested in the adults. Let's start with you."

Numbly she shook her head. "It—it wasn't me. It couldn't be me."

"Why couldn't it?"

"It's impossible."

"How can you be sure?"

"Because no one would want me dead!"

Her sharp cry seemed to take him by surprise. For a moment he was silent. Outside, on the street, a uniformed cop turned and glanced at them. Sam responded with an *everything's fine* wave of the hand, and the cop turned away again.

Nina sat clutching the rumpled hem of her gown. This man was horrid. Sam Spade without a trace of human warmth. Though it was getting hot in the car, she found herself shivering, chilled by the lack of obvious emotion displayed by the man sitting beside her.

"Can we explore this a little more?" he said.

She said nothing.

"Do you have any ex-boyfriends, Miss Cormier? Anyone who might be unhappy about your marriage?"

"No," she whispered.

"No ex-boyfriends at all?"

"Not—not in the last year."

"Is that how long you've been with your fiancé? A year?"

"Yes."

"His full name and address, please."

"Robert David Bledsoe, M.D., 318 Ocean View Drive."

"Same address?"

"We've been living together."

"Why was the wedding cancelled?"

"You'd have to ask Robert."

"So it was his decision? To call off the wedding?"

"As the expression goes, he left me at the altar."

"Do you know why?"

She gave a bitter laugh. "I've come to the earth-shattering conclusion, Detective, that the minds of men are a complete mystery to me."

"He gave you no warning at all?"

"It was just as unexpected as that..." She swallowed. "As that bomb. If that's what it was."

"What time was the wedding called off?"

"About one-thirty. I'd already arrived at the church, wedding gown and all. Then Jeremy—Robert's best man—showed up with the note. Robert didn't even have the nerve to tell me himself." She shook her head in disgust.

"What did the note say?"

"That he needed more time. And he was leaving town for a while. That's all."

"Is it possible Robert had any reason to—"

"No, it's *not* possible!" She looked him straight in the eye. "You're asking if Robert had something to do with it. Aren't you?"

"I keep an open mind, Miss Cormier."

"Robert's not capable of violence. For God's sake, he's a doctor!"

"All right. For the moment, we'll let that go. Let's look at other possibilities. I take it you're employed?"

"I'm a nurse at Maine Medical Center."

"Which department?"

"Emergency room."

"Any problems at work? Any conflicts with the rest of the staff?"

"No. We get along fine."

"Any threats? From your patients, for instance?"

She made a sound of exasperation. "Detective, wouldn't I know if I had enemies?"

"Not necessarily."

"You're trying your damn best to make me feel paranoid."

"I'm asking you to step back from yourself. Examine your personal life. Think of all the people who might not like you."

Nina sank back in the seat. *All the people who might not like me.* She thought of her family. Her older sister, Wendy, with whom she'd never been close. Her mother, Lydia, married to her wealthy snob of a husband. Her father, George, now on his fourth wife, a blond trophy bride who considered her husband's offspring a nuisance. It was one big, dysfunctional family, but there were certainly no murderers among them.

She shook her head. "No one, Detective. There's no one."

After a moment he sighed and closed his notebook. "All right, Miss Cormier. I guess that's all for now."

"For now?"

"I'll probably have other questions. After I talk to the rest of the wedding party." He opened the car door, got out, and pushed the door shut. Through the open window he said, "If you think of anything, anything at all, give me a call." He scribbled in his notebook and handed her the torn page with his name, Detective Samuel I. Navarro, and a phone number. "It's my direct line," he said. "I can also be

reached twenty-four hours a day through the police switch-
board."

"Then…I can go home now?"

"Yes." He started to walk away.

"Detective Navarro?"

He turned back to her. She had not realized how tall he
was. Now, seeing his lean frame at its full height, she
wondered how he'd ever fit in the seat beside her. "Is there
something else, Miss Cormier?" he asked.

"You said I could leave."

"That's right."

"I don't have a ride." She nodded toward the bombed-
out church. "Or a phone either. Do you think you could
give my mother a call? To come get me?"

"Your mother?" He glanced around, obviously anxious
to palm off this latest annoyance. Finally, with a look of res-
ignation, he circled around to her side of the car and opened
the door. "Come on. We can go in my car. I'll drive you."

"Look, I was only asking you to make a call."

"It's no trouble." He extended his hand to help her out.
"I'd have to go by your mother's house anyway."

"My mother's house? Why?"

"She was at the wedding. I'll need to talk to her, too.
Might as well kill two birds with one stone."

What a gallant way to put it, she thought.

He was still reaching out to her. She ignored his out-
stretched hand. It was a struggle getting out of the car,
since her train had wrapped itself around her legs, and she
had to kick herself free of the hem. By the time she'd
finally extricated herself from the car, he was regarding her
with a look of amusement. She snatched up her train and
whisked past him in a noisy rustle of satin.

"Uh, Miss Cormier?"

"What?" she snapped over her shoulder.

"My car's in the other direction."

She halted, her cheeks flushing. Mr. Detective was actually smiling now, a full-blown ate-the-canary grin.

"It's the blue Taurus," he pointed out. "The door's unlocked. I'll be right with you." He turned and headed away, toward the gathering of cops.

Nina flounced over to the blue Taurus. There she peered in disgust through the window. She was supposed to ride in *this* car? With that mess? She opened the door. A paper cup tumbled out. On the passenger floor was a crumpled McDonald's bag, more coffee cups, and a two-day-old *Portland Press Herald.* The back seat was buried under more newspapers, file folders, a briefcase, a suit jacket, and—of all things—a baseball mitt.

She scooped up the debris from the passenger side, tossed it into the back, and climbed in. She only hoped the seat was clean.

Detective Cold Fish was walking toward the car. He looked hot and harassed. His shirtsleeves were rolled up now, his tie yanked loose. Even as he tried to leave the scene, cops were pulling him aside to ask questions.

At last he slid in behind the wheel and slammed the door. "Okay, where does your mother live?" he asked.

"Cape Elizabeth. Look, I can see you're busy—"

"My partner's holding the fort. I'll drop you off, talk to your mother, and swing by the hospital to see Reverend Sullivan."

"Great. That way you can kill *three* birds with one stone."

"I do believe in efficiency."

They drove in silence. She saw no point in trying to

dredge up polite talk. Politeness would go right over this man's head. Instead, she looked out the window and thought morosely about the wedding reception and all those finger sandwiches waiting for guests who'd never arrive. She'd have to call and ask for the food to be delivered to a soup kitchen before it all spoiled. And then there were the gifts, dozens of them, piled up at home. Correction—*Robert's* home. It had never really been *her* home. She had only been living there, a tenant. It had been her idea to pay half the mortgage. Robert used to point out how much he respected her independence, her insistence on a separate identity. In any good relationship, he'd say, privilege as well as responsibility was a fifty-fifty split. That's how they'd worked it from the start. First he'd paid for a date, then she had. In fact, she'd insisted, to show him that she was her own woman.

Now it all seemed so stupid.

I was never my own woman, she thought. I was always dreaming, longing for the day I'd be Mrs. Robert Bledsoe. It's what her family had hoped for, what her mother had expected of her: to marry well. They'd never understood Nina's going to nursing school, except as a way to meet a potential mate. A doctor. She'd met one, all right.

And all it's gotten me is a bunch of gifts I have to return, a wedding gown I can't return, and a day I'll never, ever live down.

It was the humiliation that shook her the most. Not the fact that Robert had walked out. Not even the fact that she could have died in the wreckage of that church. The explosion itself seemed unreal to her, as remote as some TV melodramas. As remote as this man sitting beside her.

"You're handling this very well," he said.

Startled that Detective Cold Fish had spoken, she looked at him. "Excuse me?"

"You're taking this very calmly. Calmer than most."

"I don't know how else to take it."

"After a bombing, hysteria would not be out of line."

"I'm an ER nurse, Detective. I don't do hysteria."

"Still, this had to be a shock for you. There could well be an emotional aftermath."

"You're saying this is the calm before the storm?"

"Something like that." He glanced at her, his gaze meeting hers. Just as quickly, he looked back at the road and the connection was gone. "Why wasn't your family with you at the church?"

"I sent them all home."

"I would think you'd want them around for support, at least."

She looked out the window. "My family's not exactly the supportive type. And I guess I just...needed to be alone. When an animal gets hurt, Detective, it goes off by itself to lick its wounds. That's what I needed to do...." She blinked away an unexpected film of tears and fell silent.

"I know you don't feel much like talking right now," he said. "But maybe you can answer this question for me. Can you think of anyone else who might've been a target? Reverend Sullivan, for instance?"

She shook her head. "He's the last person anyone would hurt."

"It was his church building. He would've been near the blast center."

"Reverend Sullivan's the sweetest man in the world! Every winter, he's handing out blankets on the street. Or scrounging up beds at the shelter. In the ER, when we see patients who have no home to go to, he's the one we call."

"I'm not questioning his character. I'm just asking about enemies."

"He has no enemies," she said flatly.

"What about the rest of the wedding party? Could any of them have been targets?"

"I can't imagine—"

"The best man, Jeremy Wall. Tell me about him."

"Jeremy? There's not much to say. He went to medical school with Robert. He's a doctor at Maine Med. A radiologist."

"Married?"

"Single. A confirmed bachelor."

"What about your sister, Wendy? She was your maid of honor?"

"Matron of honor. She's a happy homemaker."

"Any enemies?"

"Not unless there's someone out there who resents perfection."

"Meaning?"

"Let's just say she's the dream daughter every parent hopes for."

"As opposed to you?"

Nina gave a shrug. "How'd you guess?"

"All right, so that leaves one major player. The one who, coincidentally, decided not to show up at all."

Nina stared straight ahead. *What can I tell him about Robert,* she thought, *when I myself am completely in the dark?*

To her relief, he didn't pursue that line of questioning. Perhaps he'd realized how far he'd pushed her. How close to the emotional edge she was already tottering. As they drove the winding road into Cape Elizabeth, she felt her calm facade at last begin to crumble. Hadn't he warned her about it? The emotional aftermath. The pain creeping through the numbness. She had held together well, had weathered two devastating shocks with little more than a few spilt tears. Now her hands were beginning to shake, and she found that every breath she took was a struggle not to sob.

When at last they pulled up in front of her mother's house, Nina was barely holding herself together. She didn't wait for Sam to circle around and open her door. She pushed it open herself and scrambled out in a sloppy tangle of wedding gown. By the time he walked up the front steps, she was already leaning desperately on the doorbell, silently begging her mother to let her in before she fell apart completely.

The door swung open. Lydia, still elegantly coiffed and gowned, stood staring at her dishevelled daughter. "Nina? Oh, my poor Nina." She opened her arms.

Automatically Nina fell into her mother's embrace. So hungry was she for a hug, she didn't immediately register the fact that Lydia had drawn back to avoid wrinkling her green silk dress. But she did register her mother's first question.

"Have you heard from Robert yet?"

Nina stiffened. *Oh please,* she thought. *Please don't do this to me.*

"I'm sure this can all be worked out," said Lydia. "If you'd just sit down with Robert and have an honest discussion about what's bothering him—"

Nina pulled away. "I'm not going to sit down with Robert," she said. "And as for an honest discussion, I'm not sure we ever had one."

"Now, darling, it's natural to be angry—"

"But aren't you angry, Mother? Can't you be angry *for* me?"

"Well, yes. But I can't see tossing Robert aside just because—"

The sudden clearing of a male throat made Lydia glance up at Sam, who was standing outside the doorway.

"I'm Detective Navarro, Portland Police," he said. "You're Mrs. Cormier?"

"The name's now Warrenton." Lydia frowned at him. "What is this all about? What do the police have to do with this?"

"There was an incident at the church, ma'am. We're investigating.

"An incident?"

"The church was bombed."

Lydia stared at him. "You're not serious."

"I'm very serious. It went off at 2:40 this afternoon. Luckily no one was hurt. But if the wedding had been held…"

Lydia paled to a sickly white. She took a step back, her voice failing her.

"Mrs. Warrenton," said Sam, "I need to ask you a few questions."

Nina didn't stay to listen. She had heard too many questions already. She climbed upstairs to the spare bedroom, where she had left her suitcase—the suitcase she'd packed for St. John Island. Inside were her bathing suits and sundresses and tanning lotion. Everything she'd thought she needed for a week in paradise.

She took off the wedding dress and carefully draped it over an armchair where it lay white and lifeless.

Useless. She looked at the contents of her suitcase, at the broken dreams packed neatly between layers of tissue paper. That's when the last vestiges of control failed her. Dressed only in her underwear, she sat down on the bed. Alone, in silence, she finally allowed the grief to sweep over her.

And she wept.

LYDIA WARRENTON was nothing like her daughter. Sam had seen it the moment the older woman opened the front door. Flawlessly made up, elegantly coiffed, her slender frame shown to full advantage by the green gown, Lydia looked like no mother of the bride he'd ever seen. There was a physical resemblance, of course. Both Lydia and Nina had the same black hair, the same dark, thickly lashed eyes. But while Nina had a softness about her, a vulnerability, Lydia was standoffish, as though surrounded by some protective force field that would zap anyone who ventured too close. She was definitely a looker, not only thin but also rich, judging by the room he was now standing in.

The house was a veritable museum of antiques. He had noticed a Mercedes parked in the driveway. And the living room, into which he'd just been ushered, had a spectacular ocean view. A million-dollar view. Lydia sat down primly on a brocade sofa and motioned him toward a wing chair. The needlepoint fabric was so pristine-looking he had the urge to inspect his clothes before sinking onto the cushion.

"A bomb," murmured Lydia, shaking her head. "I just can't believe it. Who would bomb a church?"

"It's not the first bombing we've had in town."

She looked at him, bewildered. "You mean the warehouse? The one last week? I read that had something to do with organized crime."

"That was the theory."

"This was a church. How can they possibly be connected?"

"We don't see the link either, Mrs. Warrenton. We're trying to find out if there is one. Maybe you can help us. Do you know of any reason someone would want to bomb the Good Shepherd Church?"

"I know nothing about that church. It's not one I attend. It was my daughter's choice to get married there."

"You sound as if you don't approve."

She shrugged. "Nina has her own odd way of doing things. I'd have chosen a more…established institution. And a longer guest list. But that's Nina. She wanted to keep it small and simple."

Simple was definitely not Lydia Warrenton's style, thought Sam, gazing around the room.

"So to answer your question, Detective, I can't think of any reason to bomb Good Shepherd."

"What time did you leave the church?"

"A little after two. When it became apparent there wasn't anything I could do for Nina."

"While you were waiting, did you happen to notice anyone who shouldn't have been there?"

"There were just the people you'd expect. The florists, the minister. The wedding party."

"Names?"

"There was me. My daughter Wendy. The best man— I don't remember his name. My ex-husband, George, and his latest wife."

"Latest."

She sniffed. "Daniella. His fourth so far."

"What about your husband?"

She paused. "Edward was delayed. His plane was two hours late leaving Chicago."

"So he hadn't even reached town yet?"

"No. But he planned to attend the reception."

Again, Sam glanced around the room, at the antiques. The view. "May I ask what your husband does for a living, Mrs. Warrenton?"

"He's president of Ridley-Warrenton."

"The logging company?"

"That's right."

That explained the house and the Mercedes, thought Sam. Ridley-Warrenton was one of the largest landowners in northern Maine. Their forest products, from raw lumber to fine paper, were shipped around the world.

His next question was unavoidable. "Mrs. Warrenton," he asked, "does your husband have any enemies?"

Her response surprised him. She laughed. "Anyone with money has enemies, Detective."

"Can you name anyone in particular?"

"You'd have to ask Edward."

"I will," said Sam, rising to his feet. "As soon as your husband's back in town, could you have him give me a call?"

"My husband's a busy man."

"So am I, ma'am," he answered. With a curt nod, he turned and left the house.

In the driveway, he sat in his Taurus for a moment, gazing up at the mansion. It was, without a doubt, one of the most impressive homes he'd ever been in. Not that he was all that familiar with mansions. Samuel Navarro was the son of a Boston cop who was himself the son of a

Boston cop. At the age of twelve, he'd moved to Portland with his newly widowed mother. Nothing came easy for them, a fact of life which his mother resignedly accepted.

Sam had not been so accepting. His adolescence consisted of five long years of rebellion. Fistfights in the school yard. Sneaking cigarettes in the bathroom. Loitering with the rough-and-tumble crowd that hung out in Monument Square. There'd been no mansions in his childhood.

He started the car and drove away. The investigation was just beginning; he and Gillis had a long night ahead of them. There was still the minister to interview, as well as the florist, the best man, the matron of honor, and the groom.

Most of all, the groom.

Dr. Robert Bledsoe, after all, was the one who'd called off the wedding. His decision, by accident or design, had saved the lives of dozens of people. That struck Sam as just a little bit too fortunate. Had Bledsoe received some kind of warning? Had he been the intended target?

Was that the real reason he'd left his bride at the altar?

Nina Cormier's image came vividly back to mind. Hers wasn't a face he'd be likely to forget. It was more than just those big brown eyes, that kissable mouth. It was her pride that impressed him the most. The sort of pride that kept her chin up, her jaw squared, even as the tears were falling. For that he admired her. No whining, no self-pity. The woman had been humiliated, abandoned, and almost blown to smithereens. Yet she'd had enough spunk left to give Sam an occasional what-for. He found that both irritating and amusing. For a woman who'd probably grown up with everything handed to her on a silver platter, she was a tough little survivor.

Today she'd been handed a heaping dish of crow, and she'd eaten it just fine, thank you. Without a whimper.

Surprising, surprising woman.

He could hardly wait to hear what Dr. Robert Bledsoe had to say about her.

IT WAS AFTER five o'clock when Nina finally emerged from her mother's guest bedroom. Calm, composed, she was now wearing jeans and a T-shirt. She'd left her wedding dress hanging in the closet; she didn't even want to look at it again. Too many bad memories had attached themselves like burrs to the fabric.

Downstairs she found her mother sitting alone in the living room, nursing a highball. Detective Navarro was gone. Lydia raised the drink to her lips, and by the clinking of ice cubes in the glass, Nina could tell that Lydia's hands were shaking.

"Mother?" said Nina.

At the sound of her daughter's voice, Lydia's head jerked up. "You startled me."

"I think I'll be leaving now. Are you all right?"

"Yes. Yes, of course." Lydia gave a shudder. Then she added, almost as an afterthought, "How about you?"

"I'll be okay. I just need some time. Away from Robert."

Mother and daughter looked at each other for a moment, neither one speaking, neither one knowing what to say. This was the way things had always been between them. Nina had grown up hungry for affection. Her mother had always been too self-absorbed to grant it. And this was the result: the silence of two women who scarcely knew or understood each other. The distance between them couldn't be measured by years, but by universes.

Nina watched her mother take another deep swallow of her drink. "How did it go?" she asked. "With you and that detective?"

Lydia shrugged. "What's there to say? He asked questions, I answered them."

"Did he tell you anything? About who might have done it?"

"No. He was tight as a clam. Not much in the way of charm."

Nina couldn't disagree. She'd known ice cubes that were warmer than Sam Navarro. But then, the man was just doing his job. He wasn't paid to be charming.

"You can stay for dinner, if you'd like," said Lydia. "Why don't you? I'll have the cook—"

"That's all right, Mother. Thank you, anyway."

Lydia looked up at her. "It's because of Edward, isn't it?"

"No, Mother. Really."

"That's why you hardly ever visit. Because of him. I wish you *could* get to like him." Lydia sighed and looked down at her drink. "He's been very good to me, very generous. You have to grant him that much."

When Nina thought of her stepfather, *generous* was not the first adjective that came to mind. No, *ruthless* would be the word she'd choose. Ruthless and controlling. She didn't want to talk about Edward Warrenton.

She turned and started toward the door. "I have to get home and pack my things. Since it's obvious I'll be moving out."

"Couldn't you and Robert patch things up somehow?"

"After today?" Nina shook her head.

"If you just tried harder? Maybe it's something you could talk about. Something you could change."

"Mother. Please."

Lydia sank back. "Anyway," she said, "you *are* invited to dinner. For what it's worth."

"Maybe some other time," Nina said softly. "Bye, Mother."

She heard no answer as she walked out the front door.

Her Honda was parked at the side of the house, where she'd left it that morning. The morning of what should have been her wedding. How proudly Lydia had smiled at her as they'd sat together in the limousine! It was the way a mother *should* look at her daughter. The way Lydia never had before.

And probably never would again.

That ride to the church, the smiles, the laughter, seemed a lifetime away. She started the Honda and pulled out of her mother's driveway.

In a daze she drove south, toward Hunts Point. Toward Robert's house. What had been *their* house. The road was winding, and she was functioning on automatic pilot, steering without thought along the curves. What if Robert hadn't really left town? she thought. What if he's home? What would they say to each other?

Try: goodbye.

She gripped the steering wheel and thought of all the things she'd *like* to tell him. All the ways she felt used and betrayed. *A whole year* kept going through her head. *One whole bloody year of my life.*

Only as she swung past Smugglers Cove did she happen to glance in the rearview mirror. A black Ford was behind her. The same Ford that had been there a few miles back, near Delano Park. At any other time, she would have thought nothing of it. But today, after the possibilities Detective Navarro had raised...

She shook off a vague sense of uneasiness and kept driving. She turned onto Ocean House Drive.

The Ford did too. There was no reason for alarm. Ocean House Drive was, after all, a main road in the neighborhood. Another driver might very well have reason to turn onto it as well.

Just to ease her anxiety, she took the left turnoff, toward Peabbles Point. It was a lonely road, not heavily traveled. Here's where she and the Ford would surely part company.

The Ford took the same turnoff.

Now she was getting frightened.

She pressed the accelerator. The Honda gained speed. At fifty miles per hour, she knew she was taking the curves too fast, but she was determined to lose the Ford. Only she wasn't losing him. He had sped up, too. In fact, he was gaining on her.

With a sudden burst of speed, the Ford roared up right beside her. They were neck and neck, taking the curves in parallel.

He's trying to run me off the road! she thought.

She glanced sideways, but all she could see through the other car's tinted window was the driver's silhouette. *Why are you doing this?* she wanted to scream at him. *Why?*

The Ford suddenly swerved toward her. The thump of the other car's impact almost sent the Honda spinning out of control. Nina fought to keep her car on course.

Her fingers clamped more tightly around the wheel. Damn this lunatic! She had to shake him off.

She hit the brakes.

The Ford shot ahead—only momentarily. It quickly slowed as well and was back beside her, swerving, bumping.

She managed another sideways glance. To her surprise, the Ford's passenger window had been rolled down. She caught a glimpse of the driver—a male. Dark hair. Sunglasses.

In the next instant her gaze shot forward to the road, which crested fifty yards ahead.

Another car had just cleared the crest and was barreling straight toward the Ford.

Tires screeched. Nina felt one last violent thump, felt the sting of shattering glass against her face. Then suddenly she was soaring sideways.

She never lost consciousness. Even as the Honda flew off the road. Even as it tumbled over and over across shrubbery and saplings.

It came to a rest, upright, against a maple tree.

Though fully awake, Nina could not move for a moment. She was too stunned to feel pain, or even fear. All she felt was amazement that she was still alive.

Then, gradually, an awareness of discomfort seeped through the layers of shock. Her chest hurt, and her shoulder. It was the seat belt. It had saved her life, but it had also bruised her ribs.

Groaning, she pressed the belt release and felt herself collapse forward, against the steering wheel.

"Hey! Hey, lady!"

Nina turned to see a face anxiously peering through the window. It was an elderly man. He yanked open her door. "Are you all right?" he asked.

"I'm—I think so."

"I'd better call an ambulance."

"No, I'm fine. Really, I am." She took a deep breath. Her chest was sore, but that seemed to be her only injury. With the old man's help, she climbed out of the car. Though a little unsteady, she was able to stand. She was shocked by the damage.

Her car was a mess. The driver's door had been bashed in, the window was shattered, and the front fender was peeled off entirely.

She turned and glanced toward the road. "There was another car," she said. "A black one—"

"You mean that damn fool who tried to pass you?"

"Where is it?"

"Took off. You oughta report that fella. Probably drunk as a skunk."

Drunk? Nina didn't think so. Shivering, she hugged herself and stared at the road, but she saw no sign of another car.

The black Ford had vanished.

Three

Gordon Gillis looked up from his burger and fries. "Anything interesting?" he asked.

"Not a damn thing." Sam hung his jacket up on the coatrack and sank into a chair behind his desk, where he sat wearily rubbing his face.

"How's the minister doing?"

"Fine, so far. Doctors doubt it's a heart attack. But they'll keep him in for a day, just to be sure."

"He didn't have any ideas about the bombing?"

"Claims he has no enemies. And everyone I talked to seems to agree that Reverend Sullivan is a certifiable saint." Groaning, Sam leaned back. "How 'bout you?"

Gillis peeled off the hamburger wrapper and began to eat as he talked. "I interviewed the best man, the matron of honor and the florist. No one saw anything."

"What about the church janitor?"

"We're still trying to locate him. His wife says he usually gets home around six. I'll send Cooley over to talk to him."

"According to Reverend Sullivan, the janitor opens the front doors at 7:00 a.m. And the doors stay open all day. So anyone could've walked in and left a package."

"What about the night before?" asked Gillis. "What time did he lock the doors?"

"The church secretary usually locks up. She's a part-timer. Would've done it around 6:00 p.m. Unfortunately, she left for vacation this morning. Visiting family in Massachusetts. We're still trying to get hold of..." He paused.

Gillis's telephone was ringing. Gillis turned to answer it. "Yeah, what's up?"

Sam watched as his partner scribbled something on a notepad, then passed it across the desk. *Trundy Point Road* was written on the paper.

A moment later, Gillis said, "We'll be there," and hung up. He was frowning.

"What is it?" asked Sam.

"Report just came in from one of the mobile units. It's about the bride. The one at the church today."

"Nina Cormier?"

"Her car just went off the road near Trundy Point."

Sam sat up straight in alarm. "Is she all right?"

"She's fine. They wouldn't have called us at all, but she insisted they notify us."

"For an accident? Why?"

"She says it wasn't an accident. She says someone tried to run her off the road."

HER RIBS HURT, her shoulder was sore, and her face had a few cuts from flying glass. But at least her head was perfectly clear. Clear enough for her to recognize the man stepping out of that familiar blue Taurus that had just pulled up at the scene. It was that sullen detective, Sam Navarro. He didn't even glance in her direction.

Through the gathering dusk, Nina watched as he spoke to a patrolman. They conversed for a few moments. Then, together, the two men tramped through the underbrush to view the remains of her car. As Sam paced a slow circle around the battered Honda, Nina was reminded of a stalking cat. He moved with an easy, feline grace, his gaze focused in complete concentration. At one point he stopped and crouched to look at something on the ground. Then he rose to his feet and peered more closely at the driver's window. Or what was left of the window. He prodded the broken glass, then opened the door and climbed into the front seat. What on earth was he looking for? She could see his dark hair bobbing in and out of view. Now he seemed to be crawling all over the interior, and into the back seat. It was a good thing she had nothing to hide in there. She had no doubt that the sharp-eyed Detective Navarro could spot contraband a mile away.

At last he reemerged from her car, his hair tousled, his trousers wrinkled. He spoke again to the patrolman. Then he turned and looked in her direction.

And began to walk toward her.

At once she felt her pulse quickening. Something about this man both fascinated and frightened her. It was more than just his physical presence, which was impressive enough. It was also the way he looked at her, with a gaze that was completely neutral. That inscrutability unnerved her. Most men seemed to find Nina attractive, and they would at least make an attempt to be friendly.

This man seemed to regard her as just another homicide

victim in the making. Worth his intellectual interest, but that was all.

She straightened her back and met his gaze without wavering as he approached.

"Are you all right?" he asked.

"A few bruises. A few cuts. That's all."

"You're sure you don't want to go to the ER? I can drive you."

"I'm fine. I'm a nurse, so I think I'd know."

"They say doctors and nurses make the worst patients. I'll drive you to the hospital. Just to be sure."

She gave a disbelieving laugh. "That sounds like an order."

"As a matter of fact, it is."

"Detective, I really think I'd know if I was..."

She was talking to his back. The man had actually turned his *back* to her. He was already walking away, toward his car. *"Detective!"* she called.

He glanced over his shoulder. "Yes?"

"I don't— This isn't—" She sighed. "Oh, never mind," she muttered, and followed him to his car. There was no point arguing with the man. He'd just turn his back on her again. As she slid into the passenger seat, she felt a sharp stab of pain in her chest. Maybe he was right after all. She knew it could take hours, or even days, for injuries to manifest themselves. She hated to admit it, but Mr. Personality was probably right about this trip to the ER.

She was too uncomfortable to say much as they drove to the hospital. It was Sam who finally broke the silence.

"So, can you tell me what happened?" he asked.

"I already gave a statement. It's all in the police report. Someone ran me off the road."

"Yes, a black Ford, male driver. Maine license plate."

"Then you've been told the details."

"The other witness said he thought it was a drunk driver trying to pass you on the hill. He didn't think it was deliberate."

She shook her head. "I don't know what to think anymore."

"When did you first see the Ford?"

"Somewhere around Smugglers Cove, I guess. I noticed that it seemed to be following me."

"Was it weaving? Show any signs of driver impairment?"

"No. It was just...following me."

"Could it have been behind you earlier?"

"I'm not sure."

"Is it possible it was there when you left your mother's house?"

She frowned at him. He wasn't looking at her, but was staring straight ahead. The tenor of his questions had taken a subtle change of course. He had started out sounding noncommittal. Maybe even skeptical. But this last question told her he was considering a possibility other than a drunk driver. A possibility that left her suddenly chilled.

"Are you suggesting he was waiting for me?"

"I'm just exploring the possibilities."

"The other policeman thought it was a drunk driver."

"He has his opinion."

"What's your opinion?"

He didn't answer. He just kept driving in that maddeningly calm way of his. Did the man ever show any emotion? Once, just once, she'd like to see something get under that thick skin of his.

"Detective Navarro," she said. "I pay taxes. I pay your salary. I think I deserve more than just a brush-off."

"Oh. The old civil servant line."

"I'll use whatever line it takes to get an answer out of you!"

"I'm not sure you want to hear my answer."

"Why wouldn't I?"

"I made a brief inspection of your car. What I found there backs up quite a bit of what you just told me. There were black paint chips on the driver's side, indicating that the vehicle that rammed yours was, indeed, black."

"So I'm not color blind."

"I also noticed that the driver's window was shattered. And that the breakage was in a starburst pattern. Not what I'd expect for a rollover accident."

"That's because the window was already broken when I went off the road."

"How do you know?"

"I remember I felt flying glass. That's how I cut my face. When the glass hit me. That was *before* I rolled over."

"Are you sure?" He glanced at her. "Absolutely sure?"

"Yes. Does it make a difference?"

He let out a breath. "It makes a lot of difference," he said softly. "It also goes along with what I found in your car."

"*In* my car?" Perplexed, she shook her head. "What, exactly, did you find?"

"It was in the right passenger door—the door that was jammed against the tree. The metal was pretty crumpled; that's why the other cops didn't notice it. But I knew it was there somewhere. And I found it."

"Found what?"

"A bullet hole."

Nina felt the blood drain from her face. She couldn't speak; she could only sit in shocked silence, her world rocked by the impact of his words.

He continued talking, his tone matter-of-fact. Chillingly so. *He's not human,* she thought. *He's a machine. A robot.*

"The bullet must have hit your window," he said, "just to the rear of your head. That's why the glass shattered. Then the bullet passed at a slightly forward angle, missed you completely, and made a hole in the plastic molding of the opposite door, where it's probably still lodged. It'll be retrieved. By tonight, we'll know the caliber. And possibly the make of the gun. What I still don't know—what *you'll* have to tell me—is why someone's trying to kill you."

She shook her head. "It's a mistake."

"This guy's going to a lot of trouble. He's bombed a church. Tailed you. Shot at you. There's no mistake."

"There has to be!"

"Think of every possible person who might want to hurt you. Think, Nina."

"I told you, I don't have any enemies!"

"You must have."

"I don't! I don't…." She gave a sob and clutched her head in her hands. "I don't," she whispered.

After a long silence he said, gently, "I'm sorry. I know how hard it is to accept—"

"You *don't* know." She raised her head and looked at him. "You have no idea, Detective. I've always thought people liked me. Or—at least—they didn't *hate* me. I try so hard to get along with everyone. And now you're telling me there's someone out there—someone who wants to…" She swallowed and stared ahead, at the darkening road.

Sam let the silence stretch on between them. He knew she was in too fragile a state right now to press her with more questions. And he suspected she was hurting more, both physically and emotionally, than she was letting on. Judging by the condition of her car, her body had taken a brutal beating this afternoon.

In the ER, he paced the waiting room while Nina was examined by the doctor on duty. A few X rays later, she emerged looking even more pale than when she'd entered. It was reality sinking in, he thought. The danger was genuine, and she couldn't deny it any longer.

Back in his car, she sat in numb silence. He kept glancing sideways at her, waiting for her to burst into tears, into hysteria, but she remained unnervingly quiet. It concerned him. This wasn't healthy.

He said, "You shouldn't be alone tonight. Is there somewhere you can go?"

Her response was barely a shrug.

"Your mother's?" he suggested. "I'll take you home to pack a suitcase and—"

"No. Not my mother's," she murmured.

"Why not?"

"I…don't want to make things…uncomfortable for her."

"For *her?*" He frowned. "Pardon me for asking this, but isn't that what mothers are for? To pick us up and dust us off?"

"My mother's marriage isn't…the most supportive one around."

"She can't welcome her own daughter home?"

"It's not her home, Detective. It's her husband's. And he doesn't approve of me. To be honest, the feeling's mutual." She gazed straight ahead, and in that moment, she struck him as so very brave. And so very alone.

"Since the day they got married, Edward Warrenton has controlled every detail of my mother's life. He bullies her, and she takes it without a whimper. Because his money makes it all worthwhile for her. I just couldn't stand watching it any longer. So one day I told him off."

"Sounds like that's exactly what you should have done."

"It didn't do a thing for family harmony. I'm sure that's why he went on that business trip to Chicago. So he could conveniently skip my wedding." Sighing, she tilted her head back against the headrest. "I know I shouldn't be annoyed with my mother, but I am. I'm annoyed that she's never stood up to him."

"Okay. So I don't take you to your mother's house. What about dear old dad? Do you two get along?"

She gave a nod. A small one. "I suppose I could stay with him."

"Good. Because there's no way I'm going to let you be alone tonight." The sentence was scarcely out of his mouth when he realized he shouldn't have said it. It sounded too much as if he cared, as if feeling were getting mixed up with duty. He was too good a cop, too cautious a cop, to let that happen.

He could feel her surprised gaze through the darkness of the car.

In a tone colder than he'd intended, he said, "You may be my only link to this bombing. I need you alive and well for the investigation."

"Oh. Of course." She looked straight ahead again. And she didn't say another word until they'd reached her house on Ocean View Drive.

As soon as he'd parked, she started to get out of the car. He reached for her arm and pulled her back inside. "Wait."

"What is it?"

"Just sit for a minute." He glanced up and down the

road, scanning for other cars, other people. Anything at all suspicious. The street was deserted.

"Okay," he said. He got out and circled around to open her door. "Pack one suitcase. That's all we have time for."

"I wasn't planning to bring along the furniture."

"I'm just trying to keep this short and sweet. If someone's really looking for you, this is where they'll come. So let's not hang around, all right?"

That remark, meant to emphasize the danger, had its intended effect. She scooted out of the car and up the front walk in hyperspeed. He had to convince her to wait on the porch while he made a quick search of the house.

A moment later he poked his head out the door. "All clear."

While she packed a suitcase, Sam wandered about the living room. It was an old but spacious house, tastefully furnished, with a view of the sea. Just the sort of house one would expect a doctor to live in. He went over to the grand piano—a Steinway—and tapped out a few notes. "Who plays the piano?" he called out.

"Robert," came the answer from the bedroom. "Afraid I have a tin ear."

He focused on a framed photograph set on the piano. It was a shot of a couple, smiling. Nina and some blond, blue-eyed man. Undoubtedly Robert Bledsoe. The guy, it seemed, had everything: looks, money and a medical degree. And the woman. A woman he no longer wanted. Sam crossed the room to a display of diplomas, hanging on the wall. All of them Robert Bledsoe's. Groton prep. B.A. Dartmouth. M.D. Harvard. Dr. Bledsoe was Ivy League all the way. He was every mother's dream son-in-law. No wonder Lydia Warrenton had urged her daughter to patch things up.

The phone rang, the sound so abrupt and startling, Sam felt an instant rush of adrenaline.

"Should I get it?" Nina asked. She was standing in the doorway, her face drawn and tense.

He nodded. "Answer it."

She crossed to the telephone. After a second's hesitation, she picked up the receiver. He moved right beside her, listening, as she said, "Hello?"

No one answered.

"Hello?" Nina repeated. "Who is this? *Hello?*"

There was a click. Then, a moment later, the dial tone.

Nina looked up at Sam. She was standing so close to him, her hair, like black silk, brushed his face. He found himself staring straight into those wide eyes of hers, found himself reacting to her nearness with an unexpected surge of male longing.

This isn't supposed to happen. I can't let it happen.

He took a step back, just to put space between them. Even though they were now standing a good three feet apart, he could still feel the attraction. Not far enough apart, he thought. This woman was getting in the way of his thinking clearly, logically. And that was dangerous.

He looked down and suddenly noticed the telephone answering machine was blinking. He said, "You have messages."

"Pardon?"

"Your answering machine. It's recorded three messages."

Dazedly she looked down at the machine. Automatically she pressed the Play button.

There were three beeps, followed by three silences, and then dial tones.

Seemingly paralyzed, she stared at the machine. "Why?" she whispered. "Why do they call and hang up?"

"To see if you're home."

The implication of his statement at once struck her full force. She flinched away from the phone as if it had burned her. "I have to get out of here," she said, and hurried back into the bedroom.

He followed her. She was tossing clothes into a suitcase, not bothering to fold anything. Slacks and blouses and lingerie in one disorganized pile.

"Just the essentials," he said. "Let's leave."

"Yes. Yes, you're right." She whirled around and ran into the bathroom. He heard her rattling in the cabinets, collecting toiletries. A moment later she reemerged with a bulging makeup bag, which she tossed in the suitcase.

He closed and latched it for her. "Let's go."

In the car, she sat silent and huddled against the seat as he drove. He kept checking the rearview mirror, to see if they were being followed, but he saw no other headlights. No signs of pursuit.

"Relax, we're okay," he said. "I'll just get you to your dad's house, and you'll be fine."

"And then what?" she said softly. "How long do I hide there? For weeks, months?"

"As long as it takes for us to crack this case."

She shook her head, a sad gesture of bewilderment. "It doesn't make sense. None of this makes sense."

"Maybe it'll become clear when we talk to your fiancé. Do you have any idea where he might be?"

"It seems that I'm the last person Robert wanted to confide in…" Hugging herself, she stared out the window.

"His note said he was leaving town for a while. I guess he just needed to get away. From me..."

"From you? Or from someone else?"

She shook her head. "There's so much I don't know. So much he never bothered to tell me. God, I wish I understood. I could handle this. I could handle anything. If only I understood."

What kind of man is Robert Bledsoe? Sam wondered. What kind of man would walk away from this woman? Leave her alone to face the danger left in his wake?

"Whoever made that hang-up call may pay a visit to your house," he said. "I'd like to keep an eye on it. See who turns up."

She nodded. "Yes. Of course."

"May I have access?"

"You mean...get inside?"

"If our suspect shows up, he may try to break in. I'd like to be waiting for him."

She stared at him. "You could get yourself killed."

"Believe me, Miss Cormier, I'm not the heroic type. I don't take chances."

"But if he does show up—"

"I'll be ready." He flashed her a quick grin for reassurance. She didn't look reassured. If anything, she looked more frightened than ever.

For me? he wondered. And that, inexplicably, lifted his spirits. Terrific. Next thing he knew, he'd be putting his neck in a noose, and all because of a pair of big brown eyes. This was just the kind of situation cops were warned to avoid: assuming the role of hero to some fetching female. It got men killed.

It could get *him* killed.

"You shouldn't do this by yourself," she said.

"I won't be alone. I'll have backup."

"You're sure?"

"Yeah, I'm sure."

"You promise? You won't take any chances?"

"What are you, my mother?" he snapped in exasperation.

She took her keys out of her purse and slapped them on the dashboard. "No, I'm not your mother," she retorted. "But you're the cop in charge. And I need you alive and well to crack this case."

He deserved that. She'd been concerned about his safety, and he'd responded with sarcasm. He didn't even know why. All he knew was, whenever he looked in her eyes, he had the overwhelming urge to turn tail and run. Before he was trapped.

Moments later, they drove past the wrought iron gates of her father's driveway. Nina didn't even wait for Sam to open her door. She got out of the car and started up the stone steps. Sam followed, carrying her suitcase. And ogling the house. It was huge—even more impressive than Lydia Warrenton's home, and it had the Rolls-Royce of security systems. Tonight, at least, Nina should be safe.

The doorbell chimed like a church bell; he could hear it echoing through what must be dozens of rooms. The door was opened by a blonde—and what a blonde! Not much older than thirty, she was wearing a shiny spandex leotard that hugged every taut curve. A healthy sweat sheened her face, and from some other room came the thumpy music of an exercise video.

"Hello, Daniella," Nina said quietly.

Daniella assumed a look of sympathy that struck Sam as too automatic to be genuine. "Oh Nina, I'm so *sorry* about what happened today! Wendy called and told us about the church. Was anyone hurt?"

"No. No, thank God." Nina paused, as though afraid to ask the next question. "Do you think I could spend the night with you?"

The expression of sympathy faded. Daniella looked askance at the suitcase Sam was carrying. "I, uh...let me talk to your Dad. He's in the hot tub right now and—"

"Nina has no choice. She has to stay the night," said Sam. He stepped past Daniella, into the house. "It's not safe for her to be alone."

Daniella's gaze shifted to Sam, and he saw the vague spark of interest in those flat blue eyes. "I'm afraid I didn't catch your name," she said.

"This is Detective Navarro," said Nina. "He's with the Portland Bomb Squad. And this," she said to Sam, "is Daniella Cormier. My, uh...father's wife."

Stepmother was the appropriate term, but this stunning blonde didn't look like anybody's mother. And the look she was giving *him* was anything but maternal.

Daniella tilted her head, a gesture he recognized as both inquisitive and flirtatious. "So, you're a cop?"

"Yes, ma'am."

"Bomb Squad? Is that really what you think happened at the church? A bomb?"

"I'm not free to talk about it," he said. "Not while the investigation's underway." Smoothly he turned to Nina. "If you're okay for the night, I'll be leaving. Be sure to close those driveway gates. And activate the burglar alarm. I'll check back with you in the morning."

As he gave a nod of goodbye, his gaze locked with Nina's. It was only the briefest of looks, but once again he was taken by surprise at his instinctive response to this woman. It was an attraction so powerful he felt himself at once struggling to pull away.

He did. With a curt good-night, he walked out the front door.

Outside, in the darkness, he stood for a moment surveying the house. It seemed secure enough. With two other people inside, Nina should be safe. Still, he wondered whether those particular two people would be of much help in a crisis. A father soaking in a hot tub and a spandex-and-hormones stepmother didn't exactly inspire feelings of confidence. Nina, at least, was an intelligent woman; he knew she would be alert for signs of danger.

He drove back to Robert Bledsoe's house on Ocean View Drive and left the car on a side street around the corner.

With Nina's keys, he let himself in the front door and called Gillis to arrange for a surveillance team to patrol the area. Then he closed all the curtains and settled down to wait. It was nine o'clock.

At nine-thirty, he was already restless. He paced the living room, then roamed the kitchen, the dining room, the hallway. Any stalker watching the house would expect lights to go on and off in different rooms, at different times. Maybe their man was just waiting for the residents to go to bed.

Sam turned off the living room lights and went into the bedroom.

Nina had left the top dresser drawer hanging open. Sam, pacing the carpet, kept walking back and forth past that open drawer with its tempting glimpse of lingerie. Something black and silky lay on top, and one corner trailed partway out of the drawer. He couldn't resist the impulse. He halted by the dresser, picked up the item of lingerie, and held it up.

It was a short little spaghetti-strap thing, edged with lace, and designed to show a lot. An awful lot. He tossed it back in and slammed the drawer shut.

He was getting distracted again. This shouldn't be happening. Something about Nina Cormier, and his reaction to her, had him behaving like a damn rookie.

Before, in the line of duty, he'd brushed up against other women, including the occasional stunner. Women like that spandex bimbo, Daniella Cormier, Nina's stepmother. He'd managed to keep his trousers zipped up and his head firmly screwed on. It was both a matter of self-control as well as self-preservation. The women he met on the job were usually in some sort of trouble, and it was too easy for them to consider Sam their white knight, the masculine answer to all their problems.

It was a fantasy that never lasted. Sooner or later the knight gets stripped of his armor and they'd see him for what he really was: just a cop. Not rich, not brilliant. Not much of anything, in fact, to recommend him.

It had happened to him once. Just once. She'd been an aspiring actress trying to escape an abusive boyfriend; he'd been a rookie assigned to watch over her. The chemistry was right. The situation was right. But the girl was all wrong. For a few heady weeks, he'd been in love, had thought *she* was in love.

Then she'd dropped Sam like a hot potato.

He'd learned a hard but lasting lesson: romance and police work did not mix. He had never again crossed that line while on the job, and he wasn't about to do it with Nina Cormier, either.

He turned away from the dresser and was crossing to the opposite end of the room when he heard a thump.

It came from somewhere near the front of the house.

Instantly he killed the bedroom lights and reached for his gun. He eased into the hallway. At the doorway to the living room he halted, his gaze quickly sweeping the darkness.

The streetlight shone in dimly through the windows. He saw no movement in the room, no suspicious shadows.

There was a scraping sound, a soft jingle. It came from the front porch.

Sam shifted his aim to the front door. He was crouched and ready to fire as the door swung open. The silhouette of a man loomed against the backlight of the streetlamp.

"Police!" Sam yelled. *"Freeze!"*

Four

The silhouette froze.

"Hands up," ordered Sam. "Come on, *hands up!*"

Both hands shot up. "Don't hurt me!" came a terrified plea.

Sam edged over to the light switch and flipped it on. The sudden glare left both men blinking. Sam took one look at the man standing in front of him and cursed.

Footsteps pounded up the porch steps and two uniformed cops burst through the doorway, pistols drawn. "We got him covered, Navarro!" one of them yelled.

"You're right on time," muttered Sam in disgust. "Forget it. This isn't the guy." He holstered his gun and looked at the tall blond man, who was still wearing a look of terror on his face. "I'm Detective Sam Navarro, Portland Police. I presume you're Dr. Robert Bledsoe?"

Nervously Robert cleared his throat. "Yeah, that's me. What's going on? Why are you people in my house?"

"Where've you been all day, Dr. Bledsoe?"

"I've been—uh, may I put my hands down?"

"Of course."

Robert lowered his hands and glanced cautiously over his shoulder at the two cops standing behind him. "Do they, uh, really need to keep pointing those guns at me?"

"You two can leave," Sam said to the cops. "I'm all right here."

"What about the surveillance?" one of them asked. "Want to call it off?"

"I doubt anything's coming down tonight. But hang around the neighborhood. Just until morning."

The two cops left. Sam said, again, "Where've you been, Dr. Bledsoe?"

With two guns no longer pointed at his back, Robert's terror had given way to righteous anger. He glared at Sam. "First, you tell me why you're in my house! What is this, a police state? Cops breaking in and threatening homeowners? You have no authority to be trespassing on my property. I'll have your ass in a sling if you don't produce a search warrant right now!"

"I don't have a warrant."

"You don't?" Robert gave an unpleasantly triumphant laugh. "You entered my house without a warrant? You break in here and threaten me with your macho cop act?"

"I didn't break in," Sam told him calmly. "I let myself in the front door."

"Oh, sure."

Sam pulled out Nina's keys and held them up in front of Robert. "With these."

"Those—those keys belong to my fiancée! How did you get them?"

"She lent them to me."

"She *what?*" Robert's voice had risen to a yelp of

anger. "Where is Nina? She had no right to hand over the keys to my house."

"Correction, Doctor. Nina Cormier was living here with you. That makes her a legal resident of this house. It gives her the right to authorize police entry, which she did." Sam eyed the man squarely. "Now, I'll ask the question a third time. Where have you been, Doctor?"

"Away," snapped Robert.

"Could you be more specific?"

"All right, I went to Boston. I needed to get out of town for a while."

"Why?"

"What is this, an interrogation? I don't have to talk to you! In fact I *shouldn't* talk to you until I call my lawyer." He turned to the telephone and picked up the receiver.

"You don't need a lawyer. Unless you've committed a crime."

"A crime?" Robert spun around and stared at him. "Are you accusing me of something?"

"I'm not accusing you of anything. But I do need answers. Are you aware of what happened in the church today?"

Robert replaced the receiver. Soberly he nodded. "I...I heard there was some sort of explosion. It was on the news. That's why I came back early. I was worried someone might've been hurt."

"Luckily, no one was. The church was empty at the time it happened."

Robert gave a sigh of relief. "Thank God," he said softly. He stood with his hand still on the phone, as though debating whether to pick it up again. "Do the police—do you—know what caused it?"

"Yes. It was a bomb."

Robert's chin jerked up. He stared at Sam. Slowly he sank into the nearest chair. "All I'd heard was—the radio said—it was an explosion. There was nothing about a bomb."

"We haven't made a public statement yet."

Robert looked up at him. "Why the hell would anyone bomb a church?"

"That's what we're trying to find out. If the wedding had taken place, dozens of people might be dead right now. Nina told me you're the one who called it off. Why did you?"

"I just couldn't go through with it." Robert dropped his head in his hands. "I wasn't ready to get married."

"So your reason was entirely personal?"

"What else would it be?" Robert suddenly looked up with an expression of stunned comprehension. "Oh, my God. You didn't think the bomb had something to do with *me?*"

"It did cross my mind. Consider the circumstances. You cancelled the wedding without warning. And then you skipped town. Of course we wondered about your motives. Whether you'd received some kind of threat and decided to run."

"No, that's not at all what happened. I called it off because I didn't want to get married."

"Mind telling me why?"

Robert's face tightened. "Yes, as a matter of fact," he answered. Abruptly he rose from the chair and strode over to the liquor cabinet. There he poured himself a shot of Scotch and stood gulping it, not looking at Sam.

"I've met your fiancée," stated Sam. "She seems like a nice woman. Bright, attractive." *I'm sure as hell attracted to her,* he couldn't help adding to himself.

"You're asking why I left her at the altar, aren't you?" said Robert.

"Why did you?"

Robert finished off his drink and poured himself another.

"Did you two have an argument?"

"No."

"What was it, Dr. Bledsoe? Cold feet? Boredom?" Sam paused. "Another woman?"

Robert turned and glared at him. "This is none of your damn business. Get out of my house."

"If you insist. But I'll be talking to you again." Sam crossed to the front door, then stopped and turned back. "Do you know anyone who'd want to hurt your fiancée?"

"No."

"Anyone who'd want her dead?"

"What a ridiculous question."

"Someone tried to run her car off the road this afternoon."

Robert jerked around and stared at him. He looked genuinely startled. "*Nina?* Who did?"

"That's what I'm trying to find out. It may or may not be connected to the bombing. Do you have any idea at all what's going on? Who might try to hurt her?"

There was a split second's hesitation before Robert answered. "No. No one I can think of. Where is she?"

"She's in a safe place for tonight. But she can't stay in hiding forever. So if you think of anything, give me a call. If you still care about her."

Robert didn't say anything.

Sam turned and left the house.

Driving home, he used his car phone to dial Gillis. His partner, predictably, was still at his desk. "The bridegroom's back in town," Sam told him. "He claims he has no idea why the church was bombed."

"Why am I not surprised?" Gillis drawled.

"Anything new turn up?"

"Yeah. We're missing a janitor."

"What?"

"The church janitor. The one who unlocked the building this morning. We've been trying to track him down all evening. He never got home tonight."

Sam felt his pulse give a little gallop of excitement. "Interesting."

"We've already got an APB out. The man's name is Jimmy Brogan. And he has a record. Petty theft four years ago and two OUI's, that kind of stuff. Nothing major. I sent Cooley out to talk to the wife and check the house."

"Does Brogan have any explosives experience?"

"Not that we can determine. The wife swears up and down that he's clean. And he's always home for dinner."

"Give me more, Gillis. Give me more."

"That's all I have to give, unless you want me to slit open a vein. Right now I'm bushed and I'm going home."

"Okay, call it a day. I'll see you in the morning."

All the way home, Sam's mind was churning with facts. A cancelled wedding. A missing church janitor. An assassin in a black Ford.

And a bomb.

Where did Nina Cormier fit in this crazy thicket of events?

It was eleven-thirty when he finally arrived home. He let himself in the front door, stepped into the house, and turned on the lights. The familiar clutter greeted him. What a god-awful mess. One of these days he'd have to clean up the place. Or maybe he should just move; that'd be easier.

He walked through the living room, picking up dirty laundry and dishes as he went. He left the dishes in the kitchen sink, threw the laundry in the washing machine, and started the wash cycle. A Saturday night, and the swinging bachelor does his laundry. Wow. He stood in his kitchen, listening to the machine rumble, thinking about all the things he could do to make this house more of a home. Furniture, maybe? It was a good, sound little house, but he kept comparing it to Robert Bledsoe's house with its Steinway piano, the sort of house any woman would be delighted to call home.

Hell, Sam wouldn't know what to do with a woman even if one was crazy enough to move in with him. He'd been a bachelor too long, alone too long. There'd been the occasional woman, of course, but none of them had ever lasted. Too often, he had to admit, the fault lay with him. Or with his work. They couldn't understand why any man in his right mind would actually choose to stay with this insane job of bombs and bombers. They took it as a personal affront that he wouldn't quit the job and chose *them* instead.

Maybe he'd just never found a woman who made him *want* to quit.

And this is the result, he thought, gazing wearily at the basket of unfolded clothes. The swinging bachelor life.

He left the washing machine to finish its cycle and headed off to bed.

As usual, alone.

THE LIGHTS WERE ON at 318 Ocean View Drive. Someone was home. The Cormier woman? Robert Bledsoe? Or both of them?

Driving slowly past the house in his green Jeep Cherokee, he took a good long look at the house. He noted the dense shrubbery near the windows, the shadow of pine and birch trees ringing both edges of the property. Plenty of cover. Plenty of concealment.

Then he noticed the unmarked car parked a block away. It was backlit by a streetlamp, and he could see the silhouettes of two men sitting inside. *Police,* he thought. They were watching the house.

Tonight was not the time to do it.

He rounded the corner and drove on.

This matter could wait. It was only a bit of cleanup, a loose end that he could attend to in his spare time.

He had other, more important work to complete, and only a week in which to do it.

He drove on, toward the city.

AT 9:00 a.m., the guards came to escort Billy "The Snowman" Binford from his jail cell.

His attorney, Albert Darien, was waiting for him. Through the Plexiglas partition separating the two men, Billy could see Darien's grim expression and he knew that the news was not good. Billy sat down opposite his attorney. The guard wasn't standing close enough to catch their conversation, but Billy knew better than to speak freely. That stuff about attorney-client confidentiality was a bunch of bull. If the feds or the D.A. wanted you bad enough, they'd plant a bug on anyone, even your priest. It was outrageous, how they'd violate a citizen's rights.

"Hello, Billy," said Darien through the speaker phone. "How're they treating you?"

"Like a sultan. How the hell d'you *think* they're treating me? You gotta get me a few favors, Darien. A private TV. I'd like a private TV."

"Billy, we got problems."

Billy didn't like the tone of Darien's voice. "What problems?" he asked.

"Liddell's not even going to discuss a plea bargain. He's set on taking this to trial. Any other D.A.'d save himself the trouble, but I think Liddell's using you as a stepping stone to Blaine House."

"Liddell's running for governor?"

"He hasn't announced it. But if he puts you away, he'll be golden. And Billy, to be honest, he's got more than enough to put you away."

Billy leaned forward and glared through the Plexiglas at his attorney. "That's what I pay *you* for. So what the hell're you doing about the situation?"

"They've got too much. Hobart's turned state's witness."

"Hobart's a sleazeball. It'll be a piece of cake to discredit him."

"They've got your shipping records. It's all on paper, Billy."

"Okay, then let's try again with a plea bargain. Anything. Just keep my time in here short."

"I told you, Liddell's nixed a plea bargain."

Billy paused. Softly he said, "Liddell can be taken care of."

Darien stared at him. "What do you mean?"

"You just get me a deal. Don't worry about Liddell. I'm taking care of—"

"I don't want to know about it." Darien sat back, his hands suddenly shaking. "I don't want to know a damn thing, okay?"

"You don't have to. I got it covered."

"Just don't get me involved."

"All I want from you, Darien, is to keep this from going to trial. And get me out of here soon. You got that?"

"Yeah. Yeah." Darien glanced nervously at the guard, who wasn't paying the least bit of attention to their conversation. "I'll try."

"Just watch," said Billy. A cocky grin spread on his lips. "Next week, things'll be different. D.A.'s office will be happy to talk plea bargain."

"Why? What happens next week?"

"You don't want to know."

Darien exhaled a deep sigh and nodded. "You're right," he muttered. "I don't want to know."

NINA AWAKENED to the bass thump of aerobics dance music. Downstairs, she found Daniella stretched out on the polished oak floor of the exercise room. This morning Daniella was garbed in a shiny pink leotard, and her sleek legs knifed effortlessly through the air with every beat of the music. Nina stood watching in fascination for a moment, mesmerized by that display of taut muscles. Daniella worked hard at her body. In fact, she did little else. Since her marriage to George Cormier, Daniella's only goal in life seemed to be physical perfection.

The music ended. Daniella sprang to her feet with an easy grace. As she turned to reach for a towel, she noticed Nina standing in the doorway. "Oh. Good morning."

"Morning," said Nina. "I guess I overslept. Has Dad already left for work?"

"You know how he is. Likes to get started at the crack of dawn." With the towel, Daniella whisked away a delicate sheen of perspiration. A discomforting silence stretched between them. It always did. It was more than just the awkwardness of their relationship, the bizarre reality that this golden goddess was technically Nina's stepmother. It was also the fact that, except for their connection through George Cormier, the two women had absolutely nothing in common.

And never had that seemed more apparent to Nina than at this moment, as she stood gazing at the perfect face of this perfect blonde.

Daniella climbed onto an exercise bike and began pedaling away. Over the whir of the wheel, she said, "George had some board meeting. He'll be home for dinner. Oh, and you got two phone calls this morning. One was from that policeman. You know, the cute one."

"Detective Navarro?"

"Yeah. He was checking up on you."

So he's worried about me, thought Nina, feeling an unexpected lifting of her spirits. He'd cared enough to make sure she was alive and well. Then again, maybe he was just checking to make sure he didn't have a new corpse on his hands.

Yes, that was the likely reason he'd called.

Feeling suddenly glum, Nina turned to leave the room, then stopped. "What about the second call?" she asked. "You said there were two."

"Oh, right." Daniella, still pumping away, looked serenely over the handlebars. "The other call was from Robert."

Nina stared at her in shocked silence. "Robert called?"

"He wanted to know if you were here."

"Where is *he?*"

"At home."

Nina shook her head in disbelief. "You might have told me earlier."

"You were sound asleep. I didn't see the point of waking

you." Daniella leaned into the handlebars and began to pedal with singleminded concentration. "Besides, he'll call back later."

I'm not waiting till later, thought Nina. *I want answers now. And I want them face-to-face.*

Heart thudding, she left the house. She borrowed her father's Mercedes to drive to Ocean View Drive. He'd never miss it; after all, he kept a spare Jaguar and a BMW in the garage.

By the time she pulled into Robert's driveway, she was shaking from both anger and dread. What on earth was she going to say to him?

What was he going to say to *her?*

She climbed the porch steps and rang the doorbell. She didn't have her house keys. Sam Navarro did. Anyway, this wasn't her house any longer. It never had been.

The door swung open and Robert stood looking at her in surprise. He was wearing running shorts and a T-shirt, and his face had the healthy flush of recent exercise. Not exactly the picture of a man pining for his fiancée.

"Uh, Nina," he said. "I—I was worried about you."

"Somehow I have a hard time believing that."

"I even called your father's house—"

"What happened, Robert?" Her breath rushed out in a bewildered sigh. "Why did you walk out on me?"

He looked away. That alone told her how far apart they'd drifted. "It's not easy to explain."

"It wasn't easy for me, either. Telling everyone to go home. Not knowing why it fell apart. You could have told me. A week before. A *day* before. Instead you leave me there, holding the damn bouquet! Wondering if it was all *my* fault. Something *I* did wrong."

"It wasn't you, Nina."

"What was it, then?"

He didn't answer. He just kept looking away, unwilling to face her. Maybe afraid to face her.

"I lived with you for a whole year," she said with sad wonder. "And I don't have the faintest idea who you are." With a stifled sob, she pushed past him, into the house, and headed straight for the bedroom.

"What are you doing?" he yelled.

"Packing the rest of my things. And getting the hell out of your life."

"Nina, there's no need to be uncivilized about this. We tried to make it. It just didn't work out. Why can't we still be friends?"

"Is that what we are? Friends?"

"I like to think so. I don't see why we can't be."

She shook her head and laughed. A bitter sound. "*Friends* don't twist the knife after they stab you." She stalked into the bedroom and began yanking open drawers. She pulled out clothes and tossed them on the bed. She was beyond caring about neatness; all she wanted was to get out of this house and never see it again. Or him again. Up until a moment ago, she'd thought it still possible to salvage their relationship, to pick up the pieces and work toward some sort of life together. Now she knew there wasn't a chance of it. She didn't want *him*. She couldn't even recall what it was about Robert Bledsoe that had attracted her. His looks, his medical degree—those were things she'd considered nice but not that important. No, what she'd seen in Robert—or imagined she'd seen—was intelligence and wit and caring. He'd shown her all those things.

What an act.

Robert was watching her with a look of wounded nobility. As if this was all her fault. She ignored him and went to the closet, raked out an armful of dresses, and dumped them on the bed. The pile was so high it was starting to topple.

"Does it all have to be done right now?" he asked.

"Yes."

"There aren't enough suitcases."

"Then I'll use trash bags. And I need to take my books, too."

"Today? But you've got tons of them!"

"This week I've got tons of time. Since I skipped the honeymoon."

"You're being unreasonable. Look, I know you're angry. You have a right to be. But don't go flying off the damn handle."

"I'll fly off the handle if I *want* to!" she yelled.

The sound of a throat being cleared made them both turn in surprise. Sam Navarro stood in the bedroom doorway, looking at them with an expression of quiet bemusement.

"Don't you cops *ever* bother to knock?" snapped Robert.

"I did knock," said Sam. "No one answered. And you left the front door wide open."

"You're trespassing," said Robert. "*Again* without a warrant."

"He doesn't need a warrant," said Nina.

"The law says he does."

"Not if I invite him in!"

"You didn't invite him in. He *walked* in."

"The door was open," said Sam. "I was concerned." He looked at Nina. "That wasn't smart, Miss Cormier, driving here alone. You should have told me you were leaving your father's house."

"What am I, your prisoner?" she muttered and crossed back to the closet for another armload of clothes. "How did you track me down, anyway?"

"I called your stepmother right after you left the house. She thought you'd be here."

"Well, I am. And I happen to be busy."

"Yeah," muttered Robert. "She's really good at being busy."

Nina spun around to confront her ex-fiancé. "What's that supposed to mean?"

"I'm not the only one to blame in all this! It takes two people to screw up a relationship."

"I didn't leave *you* at the church!"

"No, but you left me. Every night, for months on end."

"What? *What?*"

"Every damn night, I was here on my own! I would have enjoyed coming home to a nice meal. But you were never here."

"They needed me on the evening shift. I couldn't change that!"

"You could've quit."

"Quit my *job?* To do what? Play happy homemaker to a man who couldn't even decide if he wanted to marry me?"

"If you loved me, you would have."

"Oh, my God. I can't believe you're turning this into my fault. I didn't *love* you enough."

Sam said, "Nina, I need to talk to you."

"Not now!" Nina and Robert both snapped at him.

Robert said to her, "I just think you should know I had my reasons for not going through with it. A guy has only so much patience. And then it's natural to start looking elsewhere."

"Elsewhere?" She stared at him with new comprehension. Softly she said, "So there was someone else."

"What do you think?"

"Do I know her?"

"It hardly makes a difference now."

"It does to *me*. When did you meet her?"

He looked away. "A while ago."

"How long?"

"Look, this is irrelevant—"

"For six months, we planned that wedding. Both of us. And you never bothered to tell me the minor detail that you were seeing another woman?"

"It's clear to me you're not rational at the moment. Until you are, I'm not discussing this." Robert turned and left the room.

"Not *rational?*" she yelled. "I'm more rational now than I was six months ago!"

She was answered by the thud of the front door as it slammed shut.

Another woman, she thought. *I never knew. I never even suspected.*

Suddenly feeling sick to her stomach, she sank down on the bed. The pile of clothes tumbled onto the floor, but she didn't even notice. Nor did she realize that she was crying, that the tears were dribbling down her cheeks and onto her shirt. She was both sick and numb at the same time, and oblivious to everything but her own pain.

She scarcely noticed that Sam had sat down beside her.

"He's not worth it, Nina," he soothed quietly. "He's not worth grieving over."

Only when his hand closed warmly over hers did she look up. She found his gaze focused steadily on her face. "I'm not grieving," she said.

Gently he brushed his fingers across her cheek, which was wet with tears. "I think you are."

"I'm not. I'm *not*." She gave a sob and sagged against him, burying her face in his shirt. "I'm not," she whispered against his chest.

Only vaguely did she sense his arms folding around her back, gathering her against him. Suddenly those arms were holding her close, wrapping tightly around her. He didn't say a thing. As always, the laconic cop. But she felt his breath warming her hair, felt his lips brush the top of her head, and she heard the quickening of his heartbeat.

Just as she felt the quickening of her own.

It means nothing, she thought. He was being kind to her. Comforting her the way he would any hurt citizen. It was what she did every day in the ER. It was her job. It was his job.

Oh, but this felt so good.

It took a ruthless act of pure will to pull out of his arms. When she looked up, she found his expression calm, his green eyes unreadable. No passion, no desire. Just the public servant, in full control of his emotions.

Quickly she wiped away her tears. She felt stupid now, embarrassed by what he'd just witnessed between her and Robert. He knew it all, every humiliating detail, and she could scarcely bear to look him in the eye.

She stood up and began to gather the fallen clothes from the floor.

"You want to talk about it?" he asked.

"No."

"I think you need to. The man you loved leaves you for another woman. That must hurt pretty bad."

"Okay, I *do* need to talk about it!" She threw a handful of clothes on the bed and looked at him. "But not with some stone-faced cop who couldn't care less!"

There was a long silence. Though he looked at her without a flicker of emotion, she sensed that she'd just delivered a body blow. And he was too proud to show it.

She shook her head. "I'm sorry. Oh God, Navarro, I'm so sorry. You didn't deserve that."

"Actually," he said, "I think I did."

"You're just doing your job. And then I go and lash out at you." Thoroughly disgusted with herself, she sat down beside him on the bed. "I was just taking it out on you. I'm so—so angry at myself for letting him make me feel guilty."

"Why guilty?"

"That's the crazy part about it! I don't know why I should feel guilty! He makes it sound as if I neglected him. But I could never quit my job, even for him. I love my job."

"He's a doctor. He must've had long hours as well. Nights, weekends."

"He worked a lot of weekends."

"Did you complain?"

"Of course not. That's his job."

"Well?" He regarded her with a raised eyebrow.

"Oh." She sighed. "The old double standard."

"Exactly. I wouldn't expect my wife to quit a job she loved, just to make dinner and wait on me every night."

She stared down at her hands, clasped in her lap. "You wouldn't?"

"That's not love. That's possession."

"I think your wife's a very lucky woman," she said softly.

"I was only speaking theoretically."

She frowned at him. "You mean...it was just a theoretical wife?"

He nodded.

So he wasn't married. That piece of information made her flush with a strange and unexpected gladness. What on earth was the matter with her?

She looked away, afraid that he might see the confusion in her eyes. "You, uh, said you needed to talk to me."

"It's about the case."

"It must be pretty important if you went to all the trouble of tracking me down."

"I'm afraid we have a new development. Not a pleasant one."

She went very still. "Something's happened?"

"Tell me what you know about the church janitor."

She shook her head in bewilderment. "I don't know him at all. I don't even know his name."

"His name was Jimmy Brogan. We spent all yesterday evening trying to track Brogan down. We know he unlocked the church door yesterday. That he was in and out of the building all morning. But no one seems to know where he went after the explosion. We know he didn't turn up at the neighborhood bar where he usually goes every afternoon."

"You said *was*. That his name *was* Jimmy Brogan. Does that mean..."

Sam nodded. "We found his body this morning. He was in his car, parked in a field in Scarborough. He died from a gunshot wound to the head. The gun was in the car with him. It had his fingerprints on it."

"A suicide?" she asked softly.

"That's the way it looks."

She was silent, too shocked to say a thing.

"We're still waiting for the crime lab report. There are a number of details that bother me. It feels too neat, too packaged. It ties up every single loose end we've got."

"Including the bombing?"

"Including the bombing. There were several items in the car trunk that would seem to link Brogan to the bomb. Detonating cord. Green electrical tape. It's all pretty convincing evidence."

"You don't sound convinced."

"The problem is, Brogan had no explosives experience that we know of. Also, we can't come up with a motive for any bombing. Or for the attack on you. Can you help us out?"

She shook her head. "I don't know anything about the man."

"Are you familiar with the name Brogan?"

"No."

"He was familiar with *you*. There was a slip of paper with your address in his car."

She stared at him. His gaze was impenetrable. It frightened her, how little she could read in his eyes. How deeply the man was buried inside the cop. "Why would he have my address?" she asked.

"You must have some link to him."

"I don't know anyone named Brogan."

"Why would he try to kill you? Run you off the road?"

"How do you know *he* did it?"

"Because of his car. The one we found his body in."

She swallowed hard. "It was black?"

He nodded. "A black Ford."

Five

Sam drove her to the morgue. Neither one of them said much. He was being guarded about what information he told her, and she was too chilled to ask for the details. All the way there, she kept thinking, *Who was Jimmy Brogan and why did he want to kill me?*

In the morgue, Sam maintained a firm grip on her arm as they walked the corridor to the cold room. He was right beside her when the attendant led them to the bank of body drawers. As the drawer was pulled out she involuntarily flinched. Sam's arm came around her waist, a steady support against the terrible sight she was about to face.

"It ain't pretty," said the attendant. "Are you ready?"

Nina nodded.

He pulled aside the shroud and stepped back.

As an ER nurse, Nina had seen more than her share of grisly sights. This was by far the worst. She took one look at the man's face—what was left of it—and quickly turned away. "I don't know him," she whispered.

"Are you sure?" Sam asked.

She nodded and suddenly felt herself swaying. At once he was supporting her, his arm guiding her away from the drawers. Away from the cold room.

In the coroner's office she sat nursing a cup of hot tea while Sam talked on the phone to his partner. Only vaguely did she register his conversation. His tone was as matter-of-fact as always, betraying no hint of the horror he'd just witnessed.

"...doesn't recognize him. Or the name either. Are you sure we don't have an alias?" Sam was saying.

Nina cupped the tea in both hands but didn't sip. Her stomach was still too queasy. On the desk beside her was the file for Jimmy Brogan, open to the ID information sheet. Most of what she saw there didn't stir any memories. Not his address nor the name of his wife. Only the name of the employer was familiar: the Good Shepherd Church. She wondered if Father Sullivan had been told, wondered how he was faring in the hospital. It would be a double shock to the elderly man. First, the bombing of his church, and then the death of the janitor. She should visit him today and make sure he was doing all right...

"Thanks, Gillis. I'll be back at three. Yeah, set it up, will you?" Sam hung up and turned to her. Seeing her face, he frowned in concern. "You all right?"

"I'm fine." She shuddered and clutched the mug more tightly.

"You don't look fine. I think you need some recovery time. Come on." He offered his hand. "It's lunchtime. There's a café up the street."

"You can think about lunch?"

"I make it a point never to skip a chance at a meal. Or would you rather I take you home?"

"Anything," she said, rising from the chair. "Just get me out of this place."

NINA PICKED LISTLESSLY at a salad while Sam wolfed down a hamburger.

"I don't know how you do it," she said. "How you go straight from the morgue to a big lunch."

"Necessity." He shrugged. "In this job, a guy can get skinny real fast."

"You must see so many awful things as a cop."

"You're an ER nurse. I would think you've seen your share."

"Yes. But they usually come to us still alive."

He wiped his hands on a napkin and slid his empty plate aside. "True. If it's a bomb, by the time I get to the scene, we're lucky to find anyone alive. If we find much of them at all."

"How do you live with it? How do you stand a job like yours?"

"The challenge."

"Really, Navarro. How do you deal with the horror?"

"My name's Sam, okay? And as for how I deal with it, it's more a question of *why* I do it. The truth is, the challenge is a lot of it. People who make bombs are a unique breed of criminal. They're not like the guy who holds up your neighborhood liquor store. Bombers are craftier. A few of them are truly geniuses. But they're also cowards. Killers at a distance. It's that combination that makes those guys especially dangerous. And it makes my job all the more satisfying when I can nail them."

"So you actually enjoy it."

"*Enjoy* isn't the right word. It's more that I can't set the puzzle aside. I keep looking at the pieces and turning them around. Trying to understand the sort of mind that could do such a thing." He shook his head. "Maybe that makes me just as much a monster. That I find it so satisfying to match wits with these guys."

"Or maybe it means you're an outstanding cop."

He laughed. "Either that or I'm as screwy as the bombers are."

She gazed across the table at his smiling face and suddenly wondered why she'd ever considered those eyes of his so forbidding. One laugh and Sam Navarro transformed from a cop into an actual human being. And a very attractive man.

I'm not going to let this happen, she thought with sudden determination. *It would be such a mistake to rebound from Robert, straight into some crazy infatuation with a cop.*

She forced herself to look away, at anything but his face, and ended up focusing on his hands. At the long, tanned fingers. She said, "If Brogan was the bomber, then I guess I have nothing to worry about now."

"If he was the bomber."

"The evidence seems pretty strong. Why don't you sound convinced?"

"I can't explain it. It's just…a feeling. Instinct, I guess. That's why I still want you to be careful."

She lifted her gaze to meet his and found his smile was gone. The cop was back.

"You don't think it's over yet," she said.

"No. I don't."

SAM DROVE NINA BACK to Ocean View Drive, helped her load up the Mercedes with a few armloads of books and clothes, and made sure she was safely on her way back to her father's house.

Then he returned to the station.

At three o'clock, they held a catch-up meeting. Sam, Gillis, Tanaka from the crime lab, and a third detective on the Bomb Task Force, Francis Cooley, were in attendance. Everyone laid their puzzle pieces on the table.

Cooley spoke first. "I've checked and rechecked the records on Jimmy Brogan. There's no alias for the guy. That's his real name. Forty-five years old, born and raised in South Portland, minor criminal record. Married ten years, no kids. He was hired by Reverend Sullivan eight years ago. Worked as a janitor and handyman around the church. Never any problems, except for a few times when he showed up late and hung over after falling off the wagon. No military service, no education beyond the eleventh grade. Wife says he was dyslexic. I just can't see this guy putting together a bomb."

"Did Mrs. Brogan have any idea why Nina Cormier's address was in his car?" Sam asked.

"Nope. She'd never heard the name before. And she said the handwriting wasn't her husband's."

"Were they having any marital troubles?"

"Happy as clams, from what she told me. She's pretty devastated."

"So we've got a happily married, uneducated, dyslexic janitor as our prime suspect?"

"Afraid so, Navarro."

Sam shook his head. "This gets worse every minute." He looked at Tanaka. "Eddie, give us some answers. Please."

Tanaka, nervous as usual, cleared his throat. "You're not going to like what I have."

"Hit me anyway."

"Okay. First, the gun in the car was reported stolen a year ago from its registered owner in Miami. We don't know how Brogan got the gun. His wife says he didn't know the first thing about firearms. Second, Brogan's car *was* the black Ford that forced Miss Cormier's Honda off the road. Paint chips match, both ways. Third, the items in the trunk are the same elements used in the church bombing. Two-inch-wide green electrical tape. Identical detonator cord."

"That's Vincent Spectre's signature," said Gillis. "Green electrical tape."

"Which means we're probably dealing with an apprentice of Spectre's. Now here's something else you're not going to like. We just got back the preliminary report from the coroner. The corpse had no traces of gunpowder on his hand. Now, that's not necessarily conclusive, since powder can rub off, but it does argue against a self-inflicted wound. What clinches it, though, is the skull fracture."

"What?" Sam and Gillis said it simultaneously.

"A depressed skull fracture, right parietal bone. Because of all the tissue damage from the bullet wound, it wasn't immediately obvious. But it did show up on X ray. Jimmy Brogan was hit on the head. *Before* he was shot."

The silence in the room stretched for a good ten seconds. Then Gillis said, "And I almost bought it. Lock, stock and barrel."

"He's good," said Sam. "But not good enough." He looked at Cooley. "I want more on Brogan. I want you and your team to get the names of every friend, every acquaintance Brogan had. Talk to them all. It looks like our janitor got mixed up with the wrong guy. Maybe someone knows something, saw something."

"Won't the boys in Homicide be beating those bushes?"

"We'll beat 'em as well. They may miss something. And don't get into any turf battles, okay? We're not trying to steal their glory. We just want the bomber."

Cooley sighed and rose to his feet. "Guess it's back to the ol' widow Brogan."

"Gillis," said Sam, "I need you to talk to the best man and the matron of honor again. See if they have any links to Brogan. Or recognize his photo. I'll go back to the hospital and talk to Reverend Sullivan. And I'll talk to Dr. Bledsoe as well."

"What about the bride?" asked Gillis.

"I've pressed the questions a couple times already. She denies knowing anything about him."

"She seems to be the center of it all."

"I know. And she hasn't the foggiest idea why. But maybe her ex-bridegroom does."

The meeting broke up and everyone headed off to their respective tasks. It would take teamwork to find this bomber, and although he had good people working with him, Sam knew they were stretched thin. Since that rookie cop's death in the warehouse blast a week ago, Homicide had stepped into the investigation, and they were sucking up men and resources like crazy. As far as Homicide was concerned, the Bomb Task Force was little more than a squad of "techies"—the guys you called in when you didn't want your own head blown off.

The boys in Homicide were smart enough.

But the boys in Bombs were smarter.

That's why Sam himself drove out to Maine Medical

Center to reinterview Reverend Sullivan. This latest information on Jimmy Brogan's death had opened up a whole new range of possibilities. Perhaps Brogan had been a completely innocent patsy. Perhaps he'd witnessed something—and had mentioned it to the minister.

At the hospital, Sam learned that Reverend Sullivan had been transferred out of Intensive Care that morning. A heart attack had been ruled out, and Sullivan was now on a regular ward.

When Sam walked in the man's room, he found the minister sitting up in bed, looking glum. There was a visitor there already—Dick Yeats of Homicide. Not one of Sam's favorite people.

"Hey, Navarro," said Yeats in that cocky tone of his. "No need to spin your wheels here. We're on the Brogan case."

"I'd like to talk to Reverend Sullivan myself."

"He doesn't know anything helpful."

"Nevertheless," said Sam, "I'd like to ask my own questions."

"Suit yourself," Yeats said as he headed out the door. "Seems to me, though, that you boys in Bombs could make better use of your time if you'd let Homicide do its job."

Sam turned to the elderly minister, who was looking very unhappy about talking to yet another cop.

"I'm sorry, Reverend," said Sam. "But I'm afraid I'm going to have to ask you some more questions."

Reverend Sullivan sighed, the weariness evident in his lined face. "I can't tell you more than I already have."

"You've been told about Brogan's death?"

"Yes. That policeman—that Homicide person—"

"Detective Yeats."

"He was far more graphic than necessary. I didn't need all the...details."

Sam sat down in a chair. The minister's color was better today, but he still looked frail. The events of the last twenty-four hours must be devastating for him. First the destruction of his church building, and then the violent death of his handyman. Sam hated to flog the old man with yet more questions, but he had no choice.

Unfortunately, he could elicit no new answers. Reverend Sullivan knew nothing about Jimmy Brogan's private life. Nor could he think of a single reason why Brogan, or anyone else for that matter, would attack the Good Shepherd Church. There had been minor incidents, of course. A few acts of vandalism and petty theft. That's why he had started locking the church doors at night, a move that grieved him deeply as he felt churches should be open to those in need, day or night. But the insurance company had insisted, and so Reverend Sullivan had instructed his staff to lock up every evening at 6:00 p.m., and reopen every morning at 7:00 a.m.

"And there've been no acts of vandalism since?" asked Sam.

"None whatsoever," affirmed the minister. "That is, until the bomb."

This was a dead end, thought Sam. Yeats was right. He was just spinning his wheels.

As he rose to leave, there was a knock on the door. A heavyset woman poked her head in the room.

"Reverend Sullivan?" she said. "Is this a good time to visit?"

The gloom on the minister's face instantly transformed

to a look of relief. Thankfulness. "Helen! I'm so glad you're back! Did you hear what happened?"

"On the television, this morning. As soon as I saw it, I packed my things and started straight back for home." The woman, carrying a bundle of carnations, crossed to the bed and gave Reverend Sullivan a tearful hug. "I just saw the church. I drove right past it. Oh, what a mess."

"You don't know the worst of it," said Reverend Sullivan. He swallowed. "Jimmy's dead."

"Dear God." Helen pulled back in horror. "Was it…in the explosion?"

"No. They're saying he shot himself. I didn't even know he had a gun."

Helen took an unsteady step backward. At once Sam grasped her ample arm and guided her into the chair from which he'd just risen. She sat quivering, her face white with shock.

"Excuse me, ma'am," said Sam gently. "I'm Detective Navarro, Portland Police. May I ask your full name?"

She swallowed. "Helen Whipple."

"You're the church secretary?"

She looked up at him with dazed eyes. "Yes. Yes."

"We've been trying to contact you, Miss Whipple."

"I was—I was at my sister's house. In Amherst." She sat twisting her hands together, shaking her head. "I can't believe this. I saw Jimmy only yesterday. I can't believe he's gone."

"You saw Brogan? What time?"

"It was in the morning. Just before I left town." She began digging in her purse, desperately fishing for tissues. "I stopped in to pay a few bills before I left."

"Did you two speak?"

"Naturally. Jimmy's such…" She gave a soft sob. "*Was* such…a friendly man. He was always coming up to the office to chat. Since I was leaving on vacation, and Reverend Sullivan wasn't in yet. I asked Jimmy to do a few things for me."

"What things?"

"Oh, there was so much confusion. The wedding, you know. The florist kept popping in to use the phone. The men's bathroom sink was leaking and we needed some plumbing done quick. I had to give Jimmy some last minute instructions. Everything from where to put the wedding gifts to which plumber to call. I was so relieved when Reverend Sullivan arrived, and I could leave."

"Excuse me, ma'am," Sam cut in. "You said something about wedding gifts."

"Yes. It's a nuisance, how some people have gifts delivered to the church instead of the bride's home."

"How many gifts arrived at the church?"

"There was only one. Jimmy—oh, poor Jimmy. It's so unfair. A wife and all…"

Sam fought to maintain his patience. "What about the gift?"

"Oh. That. Jimmy said a man brought it by. He showed it to me. Very nicely wrapped, with all these pretty silver bells and foil ribbons."

"Mrs. Whipple," Sam interrupted again. "What happened to that gift?"

"Oh, I don't know. I told Jimmy to give it to the bride's mother. I assume that's what he did."

"But the bride's mother hadn't arrived yet, right? So what would Jimmy do with it?"

Helplessly Helen Whipple shrugged her shoulders. "I

suppose he'd leave it where she'd be sure to find it. In the front pew."

The front pew. The center of the blast.

Sam said, sharply, "Who was the gift addressed to?"

"The bride and groom, of course."

"Dr. Bledsoe and his fiancée?"

"Yes. That was on the card. Dr. and Mrs. Robert Bledsoe."

IT WAS STARTING to come together now, Sam thought as he got back in his car. The method of delivery. The time of planting. But the target wasn't quite clear yet. Was Nina Cormier or Robert Bledsoe supposed to die? Or was it both of them?

Nina, he knew, had no answers, no knowledge of any enemies. She couldn't help him.

So Sam drove to Ocean View Drive, to Robert Bledsoe's house. This time Bledsoe was damn well going to answer some questions, the first two being: Who was the other woman he'd been seeing, and was she jealous enough to sabotage her lover's wedding—and kill off a dozen people in the process?

Two blocks before he got there, he knew something was wrong. There were police lights flashing ahead and spectators gathered on the sidewalks.

Sam parked the car and quickly pushed his way through the crowd. At the edge of Bledsoe's driveway, a yellow police tape had been strung between wooden stakes. He flashed his badge to the patrolman standing guard and stepped across the line.

Homicide Detective Dick Yeats greeted him in the driveway with his usual I'm-in-charge tone of superiority.

"Hello again, Navarro. We have it all under control."

"You have *what* under control? What happened?"

Yeats nodded toward the BMW in the driveway.

Slowly Sam circled around the rear bumper. Only then did he see the blood. It was all over the steering wheel and the front seat. A small pool of it had congealed on the driveway pavement.

"Robert Bledsoe," said Yeats. "Shot once in the temple. The ambulance just left. He's still alive, but I don't expect he'll make it. He'd just pulled into his driveway and was getting out of his car. There's a sack of groceries in the trunk. Ice cream barely melted. The neighbor saw a green Jeep take off, just before she noticed Bledsoe's body. She thinks it was a man behind the wheel, but she didn't see his face."

"A man?" Sam's head snapped up. "Dark hair?"

"Yeah."

"Oh, God." Sam turned and started toward his car. *Nina,* he thought, and suddenly he was running. A dark-haired man had forced Nina off the road. Now Bledsoe was dead. Was Nina next?

Sam heard Yeats yell, "Navarro!" By then, he was already scrambling into his car. He made a screeching U-turn and headed away from Ocean View Drive.

He drove with his emergency lights flashing all the way to George Cormier's house.

It seemed he was ringing the bell forever before anyone answered the door. Finally it swung open and Daniella appeared, her flawless face arranged in a smile. "Why, hello, Detective."

"Where's Nina?" he demanded, pushing past her into the house.

"She's upstairs. Why?"

"I need to talk to her. *Now.*" He started for the stairway, then halted when he heard footsteps creak on the landing above. Glancing up, he saw Nina standing on the steps, her hair a tumble of black silk.

She's okay, he thought with relief. *She's still okay.*

She was dressed casually in jeans and a T-shirt, and she had a purse slung over her shoulder, as if she were just about to leave the house.

As she came down the stairs, she brought with her the elusive fragrance of soap and shampoo. Nina's scent, he thought with a pleasurable thrill of recognition. Since when had he committed her fragrance to memory?

By the time she reached the bottom step, she was frowning at him. "Has something happened?" she asked.

"Then no one's called you?"

"About what?"

"Robert."

She went very still, her dark eyes focused with sudden intensity on his face. He could see the questions in her eyes, and knew she was too afraid to ask them.

He reached for her hand. It was cold. "You'd better come with me."

"Where?"

"The hospital. That's where they took him." Gently he led her to the door.

"Wait!" called Daniella.

Sam glanced back. Daniella stood frozen, staring after them in panic. "What about Robert? What happened?"

"He's been shot. It happened a short while ago, just outside his house. I'm afraid it doesn't look good."

Daniella took a step backward, as though slapped. It was her reaction, that expression of horror in her eyes, that told Sam what he needed to know. *So she was the other woman,* he thought. *This blonde with her sculpted body and her perfect face.*

He could feel Nina's arm trembling in his grasp. He turned her toward the door. "We'd better go," he said. "There may not be much time."

Six

They spent the next four hours in a hospital waiting room.

Though Nina wasn't part of the medical team now battling to save Robert's life, she could picture only too vividly what was going on at that moment in the trauma suite. The massive infusions of blood and saline. The scramble to control the patient's bleeding, to keep his pressure up, his heart beating. She knew it all well because, at other times, on other patients, she had been part of the team. Now she was relegated to this useless task of waiting and worrying. Though her relationship with Robert was irrevocably broken, though she hadn't forgiven him for the way he'd betrayed her, she certainly didn't want him hurt.

Or dead.

It was only Sam's presence that kept her calm and sane during that long evening. Other cops came and went. As the hours stretched on, only Sam stayed next to her on the couch, his hand clasping hers in a silent gesture of support. She could see that he was tired, but he didn't leave her. He stayed right beside her as the night wore on toward ten o'clock.

And he was there when the neurosurgeon came out to inform them that Robert had died on the operating table.

Nina took the blow in numb silence. She was too stunned to shed any tears, to say much more than "Thank you for trying." She scarcely realized Sam had his arm around her. Only when she sagged against him did she feel his support, steadying her.

"I'm going to take you home," he said softly. "There's nothing more you can do here."

Mutely she nodded. He helped her to her feet and guided her toward the exit. They were halfway across the room when a voice called, "Miss Cormier? I need to ask you some more questions."

Nina turned and looked at the rodent-faced man who'd just spoken to her. She couldn't remember his name, but she knew he was a cop; he'd been in and out of the waiting room all evening. Now he was studying her closely, and she didn't like the look in his eyes.

"Not now, Yeats," said Sam, nudging her to the exit. "It's a bad time."

"It's the best time to ask questions," said the other cop. "Right after the event."

"She's already told me she knew nothing about it."

"She hasn't told *me*." Yeats turned his gaze back to Nina. "Miss Cormier, I'm with Homicide. Your fiancé never regained consciousness, so we couldn't question him. That's why I need to talk to you. Where were you this afternoon?"

Bewildered, Nina shook her head. "I was at my father's house. I didn't know about it until..."

"Until I told her," filled in Sam.

"*You* did, Navarro?"

"I went straight from the crime scene to her father's house. Nina was there. You can ask Daniella Cormier to confirm it."

"I will." Yeats's gaze was still fixed on Nina. "I understand you and Dr. Bledsoe just called off the engagement. And you were in the process of moving out of his house."

Softly Nina said, "Yes."

"I imagine you must have been pretty hurt. Did you ever consider, oh…getting back at him?"

Horrified by his implication, she gave a violent shake of her head. "You don't really think that—that I had something to do with this?"

"Did you?"

Sam stepped between them. "That's enough, Yeats."

"What are you, Navarro? Her lawyer?"

"She doesn't have to answer these questions."

"Yes, she does. Maybe not tonight. But she does have to answer questions."

Sam took Nina's arm and propelled her toward the exit.

"Watch it, Navarro!" Yeats yelled as they left the room. "You're on thin ice!"

Though Sam didn't answer, Nina could sense his fury just by the way he gripped her arm all the way to the parking lot.

When they were back in his car, she said, quietly, "Thank you, Sam."

"For what?"

"For getting me away from that awful man."

"Eventually, you *will* have to talk to him. Yeats may be a pain in the butt, but he has a job to do."

And so do you, she thought with a twinge of sadness. She turned to look out the window. He was the cop again, always the cop, trying to solve the puzzle. She was merely one of the pieces.

"You're going to have to talk to him tomorrow," said Sam. "Just a warning—he can be a tough interrogator."

"There's nothing I have to tell him. I was at my father's house. You know that. And Daniella will confirm it."

"No one can knock your alibi. But murder doesn't have to be done in person. Killers can be hired."

She turned to him with a look of disbelief. "You don't think I'd—"

"I'm just saying that's the logic Yeats will use. When someone gets murdered, the number one suspect is always the spouse or lover. You and Bledsoe just broke up. And it happened in the most public and painful way possible. It doesn't take a giant leap of logic to come up with murderous intent on your part."

"I'm not a murderer. You know I'm not!"

He didn't answer. He just went on driving as though he had not registered a word.

"Navarro, did you hear me? I'm not a murderer!"

"I heard you."

"Then why aren't you saying anything?"

"Because I think something else just came up."

Only then did she notice that he was frowning at the rearview mirror. He picked up his car phone and dialed. "Gillis?" he said. "Do me a favor. Find out if Yeats has a tail on Nina Cormier. Yeah, right now. I'm in the car. Call me back." He hung up.

Nina turned and looked out the rear window, at a pair of headlights behind them. "Is someone following us?"

"I'm not sure. I do know that car pulled out behind ours when we left the hospital. And it's been there ever since."

"Your buddy in Homicide must really think I'm danger-ous if he's having me followed."

"He's just keeping tabs on his suspect."

Me, she thought, and sank back against the seat, grateful that the darkness hid her face. *Am I your suspect as well?*

He drove calmly, making no sudden moves to alarm whoever was in the car behind them. In that tense stillness, the ringing of the phone was startling.

He picked up the receiver. "Navarro." There was a pause, then he said, "You're sure?" Again he glanced in the mirror. "I'm at Congress and Braeburn, heading west. There's a dark truck—looks like a Jeep Cherokee—right behind me. I'll swing around, make a pass by Houlton. If you can be ready and waiting, we'll sandwich this guy. Don't scare him off. For now, just move in close enough to get a good look. Okay, I'm making my turn now. I'll be there in five minutes." He hung up and shot Nina a tense glance. "You pick up what's happening?"

"What *is* happening?"

"That's not a cop behind us."

She looked back at the headlights. Not a cop. "Then who is it?"

"We're going to find out. Now listen good. In a minute I'll want you down near the floor. Not yet—I don't want to make him suspicious. But when Gillis pulls in behind him, things could get exciting. Are you ready for this?"

"I don't think I have much of a choice..."

He made his turn. Not too fast—a casual change of direc-tion to make it seem as if he'd just decided on a different route.

The other car made the turn as well.

Sam turned again, back onto Congress Street. They were headed east now, going back the way they'd come.

The pair of headlights was still behind them. At 10:30 on a Sunday, traffic was light and it was easy to spot their pursuer.

"There's Gillis," Sam stated. "Right on schedule." He nodded at the blue Toyota idling near the curb. They drove past it.

A moment later, the Toyota pulled into traffic, right behind the Jeep.

"Perp sandwich," said Sam with a note of triumph. They were coming on a traffic light, just turning yellow. Purposely he slowed down, to keep the other two cars on his tail.

Without warning, the Cherokee suddenly screeched around them and sped straight through the intersection just as the light turned red.

Sam uttered an oath and hit the accelerator. They, too, lurched through the intersection just as a pickup truck barreled in from a side street. Sam swerved around it and took off after the sedan.

A block ahead, the Cherokee screeched around a corner.

"This guy's smart," muttered Sam. "He knew we were moving in on him."

"Watch out!" cried Nina as a car pulled out of a parking space, right in front of them.

Sam leaned on his horn and shot past.

This is crazy, she thought. *I'm riding with a maniac cop at the wheel.*

They spun around the corner into an alley. Nina, clutching the dashboard, caught a dizzying view of trash cans and Dumpsters as they raced through.

At the other end of the alley, Sam screeched to a halt.

There was no sign of the Cherokee. In either direction.

Gillis's Toyota squealed to a stop just behind them. "Which way?" they heard Gillis call.

"I don't know!" Sam yelled back. "I'll head east."

He turned right. Nina glanced back and saw Gillis turn left, in the other direction. A two-pronged search. Surely one of them would spot the quarry.

Four blocks later, there was still no sign of the Cherokee. Sam reached for the car phone and dialed Gillis.

"No luck here," he said. "How about you?" At the answer, he gave a grunt of disappointment. "Okay. At least you got the license number. I'll check back with you later." He hung up.

"So he did catch the number?" Nina asked.

"Massachusetts plate. APB's going out now. With any luck, they'll pick him up." He glanced at Nina. "I'm not so sure you should go back to your father's house."

Their gazes locked. What she saw, in his eyes, confirmed her fears.

"You think he was following me," she said softly.

"What I want to know is, why? There's something weird going on here, something that involves both you and Robert. You must have *some* idea what it is."

She shook her head. "It's a mistake," she whispered. "It must be."

"Someone's gone to a lot of trouble to ensure your deaths. I don't think he—or she—would mistake the target."

"She? Do you really think..."

"As I said before, murder needn't be done in person. It can be bought and paid for. And that could be what we're dealing with. I'm more and more certain of it. A professional."

Nina was shaking now, unable to answer him. Unable

to argue. The man next to her was talking so matter-of-factly. *His* life didn't hang in the balance.

"I know it's hard to accept any of this yet," he added. "But in your case, denial could be fatal. So let me lay it out for you. The brutal facts. Robert's already dead. And you could be next."

But I'm not worth killing! she thought. *I'm no threat to anyone.*

"We can't pin the blame on Jimmy Brogan," said Sam. "I think he's the innocent in all this. He saw something he shouldn't have, so he was disposed of. And then his death was set up to look like a suicide, to throw us off the track. Deflect our bomb investigation. Our killer's very clever. And very specific about his targets." He glanced at her, and she heard, in his voice, pure, passionless logic. "There's something else I learned today," he told her. "The morning of your wedding, a gift was delivered to the church. Jimmy Brogan may have seen the man who left it. We think Brogan put the parcel somewhere near the front pews. Right near the blast center. The gift was addressed specifically to you and Robert." He paused, as though daring her to argue that away.

She couldn't. The information was coming too fast, and she was having trouble dealing with the terrifying implications.

"Help me out, Nina," he urged. "Give me a name. A motive."

"I told you," she said, her voice breaking to a sob. "I don't know!"

"Robert admitted there was another woman. Do you know who that might be?"

She was hugging herself, huddling into a self-protective ball against the seat. "No."

"Did it ever seem to you that Daniella and Robert were particularly close?"

Nina went still. *Daniella?* Her father's wife? She thought back over the past six months. Remembered the evenings she and Robert had spent at her father's house. All the invitations, the dinners. She'd been pleased that her fiancé had been so quickly accepted by her father and Daniella, pleased that, for once, harmony had been achieved in the Cormier family. Daniella, who'd never been particularly warm toward her stepdaughter, had suddenly started including Nina and Robert in every social function.

Daniella and Robert.

"That's another reason," he said, "why I don't think you should go back to your father's house tonight."

She turned to him. "You think Daniella…"

"We'll be questioning her again."

"But why would she kill Robert? If she loved him?"

"Jealousy? If she couldn't have him, no one could?"

"But he'd already broken off our engagement! It was over between us!"

"Was it really?"

Though the question was asked softly, she sensed at once an underlying tension in his voice.

She said, "You were there, Sam. You heard our argument. He didn't love me. Sometimes I think he never did." Her head dropped. "For him it was definitely over."

"And for you?"

Tears pricked her eyes. All evening she'd managed not to cry, not to fall apart. During those endless hours in the hospital waiting room, she'd withdrawn so completely into numbness that when they'd told her Robert was dead, she'd registered that fact in some distant corner of her mind, but she hadn't *felt* it. Not the shock, nor the grief. She knew she *should* be grieving. No matter how much Robert had hurt her, how bitterly their affair had ended, he was still the man with whom she'd spent the last year of her life.

Now it all seemed like a different life. Not hers. Not Robert's. Just a dream, with no basis in reality.

She began to cry. Softly. Wearily. Not tears of grief, but tears of exhaustion.

Sam said nothing. He just kept driving while the woman beside him shed soundless tears. There was plenty he *wanted* to say. He wanted to point out that Robert Bledsoe had been a first-class rat, that he was scarcely worth grieving over. But women in love weren't creatures you could deal with on a logical level. And he was sure she did love Bledsoe; it was the obvious explanation for those tears.

He tightened his grip on the steering wheel as frustration surged through him. Frustration at his own inability to comfort her, to assuage her grief. The Roberts of the world didn't deserve any woman's tears. Yet they were the men whom women always seemed to cry over. The golden boys. He glanced at Nina, huddled against the door, and he felt a rush of sympathy. And something more, something that surprised him. Longing.

At once he quelled the feeling. It was yet another sign that he should not be in this situation. It was fine for a cop to sympathize, but when the feelings crossed that invisible line into more dangerous emotions, it was time to pull back.

But I can't pull back. Not tonight. Not until I make sure she's safe.

Without looking at her, he said, "You can't go to your father's. Or your mother's for that matter—her house isn't secure. No alarm system, no gate. And it's too easy for the killer to find you."

"I—I signed a lease on a new apartment today. It doesn't have any furniture yet, but—"

"I assume Daniella knows about it?"

She paused, then replied, "Yes. She does."

"Then that's out. What about friends?"

"They all have children. If they knew a killer was trying to find me…" She took a deep breath. "I'll go to a hotel."

He glanced at her and saw that her spine was suddenly stiff and straight. And he knew she was fighting to put on a brave front. That's all it was, a front. God, what was he supposed to do now? She was scared and she had a right to be. They were both exhausted. He couldn't just dump her at some hotel at this hour. Nor could he leave her alone. Whoever was stalking her had done an efficient job of dispatching both Jimmy Brogan and Robert Bledsoe. For such a killer, tracking down Nina would be no trouble at all.

The turnoff to Route 1 north was just ahead. He took it.

Twenty minutes later they were driving past thick stands of trees. Here the houses were few and far between, all the lots heavily forested. It was the trees that had first attracted Sam to this neighborhood. As a boy, first in Boston, then in Portland, he'd always lived in the heart of the city. He'd grown up around concrete and asphalt, but he'd always felt the lure of the woods. Every summer, he'd head north to fish at his lakeside camp.

The rest of the year, he had to be content with his home in this quiet neighborhood of birch and pine.

He turned onto his private dirt road, which wound a short way into the woods before widening into his gravel driveway. Only as he turned off the engine and looked at his house did the first doubts assail him. The place wasn't much to brag about. It was just a two-bedroom cottage of precut cedar hammered together three summers ago. And as for the interior, he wasn't exactly certain how presentable he'd left it.

Oh, well. There was no changing plans now.

He got out and circled around to open her door. She stepped out, her gaze fixed in bewilderment on the small house in the woods.

"Where are we?" she asked.

"A safe place. Safer than a hotel anyway." He gestured toward the front porch. "It's just for tonight. Until we can make other arrangements."

"Who lives here?"

"I do."

If that fact disturbed her, she didn't show it. Maybe she was too tired and frightened to care. In silence she waited while he unlocked the door. He stepped inside after her and turned on the lights.

At his first glimpse of the living room, he gave a silent prayer of thanks. No clothes on the couch, no dirty dishes on the coffee table. Not that the place was pristine. With newspapers scattered about and dust bunnies in the corners, the room had that unmistakable look of a sloppy bachelor. But at least it wasn't a major disaster area. A minor one, maybe.

He locked the door and turned the dead bolt.

She was just standing there, looking dazed. Maybe by the condition of his house? He touched her shoulder and she flinched.

"You okay?" he asked.

"I'm fine."

"You don't look so fine."

In fact she looked pretty pitiful, her eyes red from crying, her cheeks a bloodless white. He had the sudden urge to take her face in his hands and warm it with his touch. Not a good idea. He was turning into a sucker for women in distress, and this woman was most certainly in distress.

Instead he turned and went into the spare bedroom. One glance at the mess and he nixed that idea. It was no place to put up a guest. Or an enemy, for that matter. There was only one solution. He'd sleep on the couch and let her have his room.

Sheets. Oh Lord, did he have any clean sheets?

Frantically he rummaged in the linen closet and found a fresh set. He was on top of things after all. Turning, he found himself face-to-face with Nina.

She held out her arms for the sheets. "I'll make up the couch."

"These are for the bed. I'm putting you in my room."

"No, Sam. I feel guilty enough as it is. Let me take the couch."

Something in the way she looked at him—that upward tilt of her chin—told him she'd had enough of playing the object of pity.

He gave her the sheets and added a blanket. "It's a lumpy couch. You don't mind?"

"I've taken a lot of lumps lately. I'll hardly notice a few more."

Almost a joke. That was good. She was pulling herself together—an act of will he found impressive.

While she made up the couch, he went to the kitchen and called Gillis at home.

"We got the info on that Massachusetts plate," Gillis

told him. "It was stolen two weeks ago. APB hasn't netted the Cherokee yet. Man, this guy's quick."

"And dangerous."

"You think he's our bomber?"

"Our shooter, too. It's all tangled together, Gillis. It has to be."

"How does last week's warehouse bombing fit in? We figured that was a mob hit."

"Yeah. A nasty message to Billy Binford's rivals."

"Binford's in jail. His future's not looking so bright. Why would he order a church bombed?"

"The church wasn't the target, Gillis. I'm almost certain the target was Bledsoe or Nina Cormier. Or both."

"How does that tie in with Binford?"

"I don't know. Nina's never heard of Binford." Sam rubbed his face and felt the stubble of beard. God, he was tired. Too tired to figure anything out tonight. He said, "There's one other angle we haven't ruled out. The old crime of passion. You interviewed Daniella Cormier."

"Yeah. Right after the bombing. What a looker."

"You pick up anything odd about her?"

"What do you mean?"

"Anything that didn't sit right? Her reactions, her answers?"

"Not that I recall. She seemed appropriately stunned. What are you thinking?"

"I'm thinking Homicide should get their boys over there to question her tonight."

"I'll pass that message along to Yeats. What's your hunch?"

"She and Robert Bledsoe had a little thing going on the side."

"And she blew up the church out of jealousy?" Gillis laughed. "She didn't seem the type."

"Remember what they say about the female of the species."

"Yeah, but I can't imagine that gorgeous blonde—"

"Watch the hormones, Gillis."

His partner snorted. "If anyone better watch his hormones, it's you."

That's what I keep telling myself, thought Sam as he hung up. He paused for a moment in the kitchen, giving himself the same old lecture he'd given himself a dozen times since meeting Nina. *I'm a cop, I'm here to serve and protect. Not seduce.*

Not fall in love.

He went into the living room. At his first sight of Nina, he felt his resolve crumble. She was standing at the window, peering out at the darkness. He'd hung no curtains; here in the woods, he'd never felt the need for them. But now he realized just how open and vulnerable she was. And that worried him—more than he cared to admit.

He said, "I'd feel better if you came away from those windows."

She turned, a startled look in her eyes. "You don't think someone could have followed us?"

"No. But I'd like you to stay away from the windows all the same."

Shuddering, she moved to the couch and sat down. She'd already made the couch into a bed, and only now did he realize how tattered the blanket was. Tattered furniture, tattered linens. Those were details that had never bothered him before. So many things about his life as a bachelor had not bothered him, simply because he'd never stopped to think how much better, sweeter, his life could be. Only now, as he saw Nina sitting on his couch, did it occur to him how stark the room was. It was only the presence of this woman that gave it any life. Any warmth.

Too soon, she'd be gone again.

The sooner the better, he told himself. Before she grew on him. Before she slipped too deeply into his life.

He paced over to the fireplace, paced back toward the kitchen door, his feet restless, his instincts telling him to say something.

"You must be hungry," he said.

She shook her head. "I can't think about food. I can't think about anything except..."

"Robert?"

She lowered her head and didn't answer. Was she crying again? She had a right to. But she just sat very still and silent, as though struggling to hold her emotions in check.

He sat down in the chair across from her. "Tell me about Robert," he prompted. "Tell me everything you know about him."

She took a shaky breath, then said softly, "I don't know what to say. We lived together a year. And now I feel as if I never knew him at all."

"You met at work?"

She nodded. "The Emergency Room. Evening shift. I'd been working there for three years. Then Robert joined the ER staff. He was a good doctor. One of the best I'd ever worked with. And he was so fun to talk to. He'd traveled everywhere, done everything. I remember how surprised I was to learn he wasn't married."

"Never?"

"Never. He told me he was holding out for the best. That he just hadn't found the woman he wanted to spend his life with."

"At forty-one, he must've been more than a little picky."

Her glance held a trace of amusement. "*You're* not married, Detective. Does that make you more than a little picky?"

"Guilty as charged. But then, I haven't really been looking."

"Not interested?"

"Not enough time for romance. It's the nature of the job."

She gave a sigh. "No, it's the nature of the beast. Men don't really want to be married."

"Did I say that?"

"It's something I've finally figured out after years of spinsterhood."

"We're all rats, that kind of thing? Let's get back to one specific rat. Robert. You were telling me you two met in the ER. Was it love at first sight?"

She leaned back, and he could clearly see the remembered pain on her face. "No. No, it wasn't. At least, not for me. I thought he was attractive, of course."

Of course, thought Sam with an undeniable twinge of cynicism.

"But when he asked me out, that first time, I didn't really think it would go anywhere. It wasn't until I introduced him to my mother that I began to realize what a catch he was. Mom was thrilled with Robert. All these years, I'd been dating guys she considered losers. And here I show up with a doctor. It was more than she'd ever expected of me, and she was already hearing wedding bells."

"What about your father?"

"I think he was just plain relieved I was dating someone who wouldn't marry me for *his* money. That's always been Dad's preoccupation. His money. And his wives. Or rather, whichever wife he happens to be married to at the time."

Sam shook his head. "After what you've seen of your parents' marriages, I'm surprised you wanted to take the plunge at all."

"But that's exactly why I *did* want to be married!" She looked at him. "To make it *work*. I never had that stability in my family. My parents were divorced when I was eight, and after that it was a steady parade of stepmothers and mother's boyfriends. I didn't want to live my own life that way." Sighing, she looked down at her ringless left hand. "Now I wonder if it's just another urban myth. A stable marriage."

"My parents had one. A good one."

"Had?"

"Before my dad died. He was a cop, in Boston. Didn't make it to his twentieth year on the force." Now Sam was the one who wasn't looking at *her*. He was gazing, instead, at some distant point in the room, avoiding her look of sympathy. He didn't feel he particularly needed her sympathy. One's parents died, and one went on with life. There was no other choice.

"After my dad died, Mom and I moved to Portland," he continued. "She wanted a safer town. A town where she wouldn't have to worry about her kid being shot on the street." He gave a rueful smile. "She wasn't too happy when I became a cop."

"Why did you become a cop?"

"I guess it was in the genes. Why did you become a nurse?"

"It was definitely *not* in the genes." She sat back, thinking it over for a moment. "I guess I wanted that one-on-one sense of helping someone. I like the contact. The touching. That was important to me, that it be hands-on. Not some vague idea of service to humanity." She gave a wry smile. "You said your mother didn't want you to be a cop. Well, my mother wasn't too happy about *my* career choice, either."

"What does she have against nursing?"

"Nothing. Just that it's not an appropriate profession for her daughter. She thinks of it as manual labor, something other women do. I was expected to marry well, entertain with flair, and help humanity by hosting benefits. That's why she was so happy about my engagement. She thought I was finally on the right track. She was actually...*proud* of me for the first time."

"That's not why you wanted to marry Robert, was it? To please your mother?"

"I don't know." She looked at him with genuine puzzlement. "I don't know anymore."

"What about love? You must have loved him."

"How can I be sure of anything? I've just found out he was seeing someone else. And now it seems as if I were caught up in some fantasy. In love with a man I made up." She leaned back and closed her eyes. "I don't want to talk about him anymore."

"It's important you tell me everything you know. That you consider all the possible reasons someone wanted him dead. A man doesn't just walk up to a stranger and shoot him in the head. The killer had a reason."

"Maybe he didn't. Maybe he was crazy. Or high on drugs. Robert could have been in the wrong place at the wrong time."

"You don't really believe that. Do you?"

She paused. Then, softly, she said, "No, I guess I don't."

He watched her for a moment, thinking how very vulnerable she looked. Had he been any other man, he would be taking her in his arms, offering her comfort and warmth.

Suddenly he felt disgusted with himself. This was the wrong time to be pressing for answers, the wrong time to be doing the cop act. Yet that act was the only thing that kept him comfortably at a distance. It protected him, insulated him. From her.

He rose from the chair. "I think we both need to get some sleep."

Her response was a silent nod.

"If you need anything, my room's at the end of the hall. Sure you wouldn't rather take my bed? Give me the couch?"

"I'll be fine here. Good night."

That was his cue to retreat. He did.

In his bedroom, he paced between the closet and the dresser, unbuttoning his shirt. He felt more restless than tired, his brain moving a mile a minute. In the last two days, a church had been bombed, a man shot to death, and a woman run off the road in an apparent murder attempt. He felt certain it was all linked, perhaps even linked to that warehouse bombing a week ago, but he couldn't see the connection. Maybe he was too dense. Maybe his brain was too drunk on hormones to think straight.

It was all her fault. He didn't need or want this complication. But he couldn't seem to think about this case without lingering on thoughts of her.

And now she was in his house.

He hadn't had a woman sleeping under his roof since...well, it was longer than he cared to admit. His last fling had amounted to little more than a few weeks of lust with a woman he'd met at some party. Then, by mutual agreement, it was over. No complications, no broken hearts.

Not much satisfaction, either.

These days, what satisfaction he got came from the challenge of his work. That was one thing he could count on: the world would never run out of perps.

He turned off the lights and stretched out on the bed, but still he wasn't ready to sleep. He thought of Nina, just down the hall. Thought of what a mismatch they'd be together. And how horrified her mother would be if a cop started squiring around her daughter. If a cop even had a chance.

What a mistake, bringing her here. Lately it seemed he was making a lot of mistakes. He wasn't going to compound this one by falling in love or lust or whatever it was he felt himself teetering toward.

Tomorrow, he thought, *she's out of here.*

And I'm back in control.

Seven

Nina knew she ought to be crying, but she couldn't. In darkness she lay on the couch and thought about those months she'd lived with Robert. The months she'd thought of as stepping stones to their marriage. When had it fallen apart? When had he stopped telling her the truth? She should have noticed the signs. The avoided looks, the silences.

She remembered that two weeks ago, he'd suggested the wedding be postponed. She'd assumed it was merely bridegroom jitters. By then, the arrangements were all made, the date set in stone.

How trapped he must have felt.

Oh Robert. If only you'd come out and told me.

She could have dealt with the truth. The pain, the rejection. She was strong enough and adult enough. What she couldn't deal with was the fact that, all these months, she'd been living with a man she scarcely knew.

Now she'd never know what he really felt about her. His death had cut off any chance she had to make peace with him.

At last she did fall asleep, but the couch was lumpy and the dreams kept waking her up.

Dreams not of Robert, but of Sam Navarro.

He was standing before her, silent and unsmiling. She saw no emotion in his eyes, just that flat, unreadable gaze of a stranger. He reached out to her, as though to take her hand. But when she looked down, there were handcuffs circling her wrists.

"You're guilty," he said. And he kept repeating the word. *Guilty. Guilty.*

She awakened with tears in her eyes. Never had she felt so alone. And she *was* alone, reduced to the pitiful state of seeking refuge in the home of a cop who cared nothing at all about her. Who considered her little more than an added responsibility. An added bother.

It was a flicker of shadow across the window that drew her attention. She would not have noticed it at all, save for the fact it had passed just to the right of her, a patch of darkness moving across her line of vision. Suddenly her heart was thudding. She stared at the curtainless squares of moonlight, watching for signs of movement.

There it was again. A shadow, flitting past.

In an instant she was off the couch and running blindly up the hallway to Sam's room. She didn't stop to knock, but pushed right inside.

"Sam?" she whispered. He didn't answer. Frantic to wake him, she reached down to give him a shake, and her hands met warm, bare flesh. "Sam?"

At her touch, he awoke with such a violent start she jerked away in fright. "What?" he said. "What is it?"

"I think there's someone outside!"

At once he seemed to snap fully awake. He rolled off

the bed and grabbed his trousers from a chair. "Stay here," he whispered. "Don't leave the room."

"What are you going to do?"

She was answered by a metallic click. A gun. Of course he had a gun. He was a cop.

"Just stay here," he ordered, and slipped out of the room.

She wasn't crazy; she wasn't going to go wandering around a dark house when there was a cop with a loaded gun nearby. Chilled and shivering, she stood by the door and listened. She heard Sam's footsteps creak down the hall toward the living room. Then there was silence, a silence so deep it made every breath she took seem like a roar. Surely he hadn't left the house? He wouldn't go outside, would he?

The creak of returning footsteps made her back away from the door. She scurried to the far side of the bed. At the first glimpse of a figure entering the room, she ducked behind the mattress. Only when she heard Sam say, "Nina?" did she dare raise her head.

"Here," she whispered, suddenly feeling ridiculous as she emerged from her hiding place.

"There's no one out there."

"But I saw someone. Something."

"It could have been a deer. An owl flying past." He set his gun down on the nightstand. The solid clunk of metal on wood made her flinch. She hated guns. She wasn't sure she wanted to be anywhere near a man who owned one. Tonight, though, she didn't have a choice.

"Nina, I know you're scared. You have a right to be. But I've checked, and there's no one out there." He reached toward her. At the first touch of his hand on her arm, he gave a murmur of alarm. "You're freezing."

"I'm scared. Oh God, Sam. I'm so scared…"

He took her by the shoulders. By now she was shaking so hard she could barely form any words. Awkwardly, he drew her against him, and she settled, trembling, against his chest. If only he'd hold her. If only he'd put his arms around her. When at last he did, it was like being welcomed home. Enclosed in warmth and safety. This was not the man she'd dreamed about, not the cold, unsmiling cop. This was a man who held her and murmured comforting sounds. A man whose face nuzzled her hair, whose lips, even now, were lowering toward hers.

The kiss was gentle. Sweet. Not the sort of kiss she ever imagined Sam Navarro capable of. Certainly she never imagined being hugged by him, comforted by him. But here she was, in his arms, and she had never felt so protected.

He coaxed her, still shivering, to the bed. He pulled the covers over them both. Again, he kissed her. Again the kiss was gently undemanding. The heat of the bed, of their bodies, banished her chill. And she became aware of so many other things: the scent of his bare skin, the bristly plane of his chest. And most of all, the touch of his lips, lingering against hers.

They had their arms wrapped around each other now, and their legs were slowly twining together. The kiss had gone beyond sweetness, beyond comfort. This was transforming to lust, pure and simple, and she was responding with such a rush of eagerness it astonished her. Her lips parted, welcoming the thrust of his tongue. Through the tangle of sheets, the barrier of her clothes, she felt the undeniable evidence of his arousal burgeoning against her.

She had not meant for this to happen, had not expected

this to happen. But as their kiss deepened, as his hand slid hungrily down the curve of her waist, the flare of her hips, she knew that this had been inevitable. That for all his cool, unreadable looks, Sam Navarro harbored more passion than any man she'd ever known.

He regained control first. Without warning, he broke off the kiss. She heard his breathing, harsh and rapid, in the darkness.

"Sam?" she whispered.

He pulled away from her and sat up on the side of the bed. She watched his silhouette in the darkness, running his hands through his hair. "God," he murmured. "What am I doing?"

She reached out toward the dark expanse of his back. As her fingers brushed his skin, she felt his shudder of pleasure. He wanted her—that much she was certain of. But he was right, this was a mistake, and they both knew it. She'd been afraid and in need of a protector. He was a man alone, in need of no one, but still a man with needs. It was natural they'd seek each other's arms for comfort, however temporary it might be.

Staring at him now, at the shadow huddled at the side of the bed, she knew she still wanted him. The longing was so intense it was a physical ache.

She said, "It's not so awful, is it? What just happened between us?"

"I'm not getting sucked into this again. I can't."

"It doesn't have to mean anything, Sam. Not if you don't want it to."

"Is that how you see it? Quick and meaningless?"

"No. No, that's not at all what I said."

"But that's how it'd end up." He gave a snort of self-disgust. "This is the classic trap, you know. I want to keep you safe. You want a white knight. It's good only as long as that lasts. And then it falls apart." He rose from the bed and moved to the door. "I'll sleep on the couch."

He left the room.

She lay alone in his bed, trying to sort out the confusing whirl of emotions. Nothing made sense to her. Nothing was under her control. She tried to remember a time when her life was in perfect order. It was before Robert. Before she'd let herself get caught up in those fantasies of the perfect marriage. That was where she'd gone wrong. Believing in fantasies.

Her reality was growing up in a broken home, living with a succession of faceless stepparents, having a mother and father who despised each other. Until she'd met Robert, she hadn't expected to marry at all. She'd been content enough with her life, her job. That's what had always sustained her: her work.

She could go back to that. She *would* go back to that.

That dream of a happy marriage, that fantasy, was dead.

SAM WAS UP AT DAWN. The couch had been even more uncomfortable than he'd expected. His sleep had been fitful, his shoulder ached, and at 7:00 a.m., he was unfit for human companionship. So when the phone rang, he was hard-pressed to answer with a civil "Hello."

"Navarro, you've got some explaining to do," said Abe Coopersmith.

Sam sighed. "Good morning, Chief."

"I just got an earful from Yeats in Homicide. I shouldn't have to tell you this, Sam. Back off the Cormier woman."

"You're right. You shouldn't have to tell me. But you did."

"Anything going on between you two?"

"I felt she was in danger. So I stepped in."

"Where is she right now?"

Sam paused. He couldn't avoid this question; he had to answer it. "She's here," he admitted. "My house."

"Damn."

"Someone was following us last night. I didn't think it was prudent to leave her alone. Or unprotected."

"So you brought her to *your* house? Where, exactly, did you happen to park your common sense?"

I don't know, thought Sam. *I lost track of it when I looked into Nina Cormier's big brown eyes.*

"Don't tell me you two are involved. Please don't tell me that," said Coopersmith.

"We're not involved."

"I hope to God you're not. Because Yeats wants her in here for questioning."

"For Robert Bledsoe's murder? Yeats is fishing. She doesn't know anything about it."

"He wants to question her. Bring her in. One hour."

"She has an airtight alibi—"

"*Bring her in,* Navarro." Coopersmith hung up.

There was no way around this. Much as he hated to do it, he'd have to hand Nina over to the boys in Homicide. Their questioning might be brutal, but they had their job to do. As a cop, he could hardly stand in their way.

He went up the hall to the bedroom door and knocked. When she didn't answer, he cautiously cracked open the door and peeked inside.

She was sound asleep, her hair spread across the pillow in a luxurious fan of black. Just the sight of her, lying so peacefully in his bed, in his house, sent a rush of yearning through him. It was so intense he had to grip the doorknob just to steady himself. Only when it had passed, when he had ruthlessly suppressed it, did he dare enter the room.

She awakened with one gentle shake of the shoulder. Dazed by sleep, she looked at him with an expression of utter vulnerability, and he cleared his throat just to keep his voice steady.

"You'll have to get up," he told her. "The detectives in Homicide want to see you downtown."

"When?"

"One hour. You have time to take a shower. I've already got coffee made."

She didn't say anything. She just looked at him with an expression of bewilderment. And no wonder. Last night they had held each other like lovers.

This morning, he was behaving like a stranger.

This was a mistake, coming into her room. Approaching the bed. At once he put distance between them and went to the door. "I'm sure it'll just be routine questions," he said. "But if you feel you need a lawyer—"

"Why should I need a lawyer?"

"It's not a bad idea."

"I don't need one. I didn't do anything." Her gaze was direct and defiant. He'd only been trying to protect her rights, but she had taken his suggestion the wrong way, had interpreted it as an accusation.

He didn't have the patience right now to set her straight. "They'll be waiting for us," was all he said, and he left the room.

While she showered, he tried to scrounge together a breakfast, but could come up with only frozen French bread and a months-old box of cornflakes. Both the pantry and the refrigerator looked pretty pathetic; bachelorhood was showing, and he wasn't at all proud of it.

In disgust, he went outside to fetch the newspaper, which had been delivered to its usual spot at the end of the driveway. He was walking back toward the house when he abruptly halted and stared at the ground.

There was a footprint.

Or, rather, a series of footprints. They tracked through the soft dirt, past the living room window, and headed off among the trees. A man's shoes, thick soled. Size eleven at least.

He glanced toward the house and thought about what the man who'd made those prints could have seen last night, through the windows. Only darkness? Or had he seen Nina, a moving target as she walked around the living room?

He went to his car, parked near the front porch. Slowly, methodically, he examined it from bumper to bumper. He found no signs of tampering.

Maybe I'm paranoid. Maybe those footprints mean nothing.

He went back inside, into the kitchen, and found Nina finishing up her cup of coffee. Her face was flushed, her hair still damp from the shower. At her first look at him, she frowned. "Is something wrong?" she asked.

"No, everything's fine." He carried his cup to the sink. There he looked out the window and thought about how isolated this house was. How open those windows were to the sight of a gunman.

He turned to her and said, "I think it's time to leave."

I SHOULD HAVE TAKEN Sam's advice. I should have hired a lawyer.

That was the thought that now crossed Nina's mind as she sat in an office at the police station and faced the three Homicide detectives seated across the table from her. They were polite enough, but she sensed their barely restrained eagerness. Detective Yeats in particular made her think of an attack dog—leashed, but only for the moment.

She glanced at Sam, hoping for moral support. He gave her none. Throughout the questioning, he hadn't even looked at her. He stood at the window, his shoulders rigid, his gaze focused outside. He'd brought her here, and now he was abandoning her. The cop, of course, had his duty to perform. And at this moment, he was playing the cop role to the hilt.

She said to Yeats, "I've told you everything I know. There's nothing else I can think of."

"You were his fiancée. If anyone would know, you would."

"I don't. I wasn't even there. If you'd just talk to Daniella—"

"We have. She confirms your alibi," Yeats admitted.

"Then why do you keep asking me these questions?"

"Because murder doesn't have to be done in person," one of the other cops said.

Now Yeats leaned forward, his gaze sympathetic, his voice quietly coaxing. "It must have been pretty humiliating for you," he persisted. "To be left at the altar. To have the whole world know he didn't want you."

She said nothing.

"Here's a man you trusted. A man you loved. And for weeks, maybe months, he was cheating on you. Probably laughing at you behind your back. A man like that doesn't deserve a woman like you. But you loved him anyway. And all you got for it was pain."

She lowered her head. She still didn't speak.

"Come on, Nina. Didn't you want to hurt him back? Just a little?"

"Not—not that way," she whispered.

"Even when you found out he was seeing someone else? Even when you learned it was your own step-mother?"

She looked up sharply at Yeats.

"It's true. We spoke to Daniella and she admitted it. They'd been meeting on the sly for some time. While you were at work. You didn't know?"

Nina swallowed. In silence she shook her head.

"I think maybe you *did* know. Maybe you found out on your own. Maybe he told you."

"No."

"And how did it make you feel? Hurt? Angry?"

"I didn't know."

"Angry enough to strike back? To find someone who'd strike back *for* you?"

"I didn't know!"

"That's simply not believable, Nina. You expect us to accept your word that you knew nothing about it?"

"I didn't!"

"You *did*. You—"

"That's *enough*." It was Sam's voice that cut in. "What the hell do you think you're doing, Yeats?"

"My job," Yeats shot back.

"You're badgering her. Interrogating without benefit of counsel."

"Why should she need a lawyer? She claims she's innocent."

"She *is* innocent."

Yeats glanced smugly at the other Homicide detectives. "I think it's pretty obvious, Navarro, that you no longer belong on this investigation."

"You don't have the authority."

"Abe Coopersmith's given me the authority."

"Yeats, I don't give a flying—"

Sam's retort was cut off by the beeping of his pocket pager. Irritably he pressed the Silence button. "I'm not through here," he snapped. Then he turned and left the room.

Yeats turned back to Nina. "Now, Miss Cormier," he said. All trace of sympathy was gone from his expression. In its place was the razor-tooth smile of a pit bull. "Let's get back to the questions."

THE PAGE WAS FROM Ernie Takeda in the crime lab, and the code on the beeper readout told Sam it was an urgent message. He made the call from his own desk.

It took a few dialings to get through; the line was busy. When the usually low-key Takeda finally answered, there was an uncharacteristic tone of excitement in his voice.

"We've got something for you, Sam," said Takeda. "Something that'll make you happy."

"Okay. Make me happy."

"It's a fingerprint. A partial, from one of the device fragments from the warehouse bomb. It could be enough to ID our bomber. I've sent the print off to NCIC. It'll take a few days to run it through the system. So be patient. And let's hope our bomber is on file somewhere."

"You're right, Ernie. You've made me a happy man."

"Oh, one more thing. About that church bomb."

"Yes?"

"Based on the debris, I'd say the device had some sort of gift wrapping around it. Also, since it had no timing elements, my guess is, it was designed to be triggered on opening. But it went off prematurely. Probably a short circuit of some kind."

"You mentioned gift wrapping."

"Yeah. Silver-and-white paper."

Wedding wrap, thought Sam, remembering the gift that had been delivered that morning to the church. If the bomb was meant to explode on opening, then there was no longer any doubt who the intended victims were.

But why kill Nina? he wondered as he headed back to the conference room. Could this whole mess be attributed to another woman's jealousy? Daniella Cormier had a motive, but would she have gone so far as to hire a bomber?

What was he missing here?

He opened the office door and halted. The three homicide detectives were still sitting at the table. Nina wasn't. She was gone.

"Where is she?" Sam asked.

Yeats shrugged. "She left."

"What?"

"She got fed up with our questions, so she walked out."

"You *let* her leave?"

"We haven't charged her with anything. Are you saying we should have, Navarro?"

Sam's reply was unrepeatable. With a sudden sense of anxiety, he left Yeats and headed out the front entrance of police headquarters. He stood on the sidewalk, looking up and down the street.

Nina was nowhere in sight.

Someone's trying to kill her, he thought as he headed for his car. *I have to reach her first.*

From his car phone, he called Nina's father's house. She wasn't there. He called Robert Bledsoe's house. No answer. He called Lydia Warrenton's house. Nina wasn't there either.

On a hunch, he drove to Lydia's Cape Elizabeth home anyway. People in distress often flee home for comfort, he reasoned. Eventually, Nina might wind up at her mother's.

He found Lydia at home. But no Nina—not yet, at least.

"I haven't spoken to her since yesterday morning," said Lydia, ushering Sam into the seaview room. "I'm not sure she *would* come here."

"Do you know where she might go?" Sam asked. "Someone she might turn to?"

Lydia shook her head. "I'm afraid my daughter and I aren't very close. We never were. The truth is, she wasn't the easiest child."

"What do you mean, Mrs. Warrenton?"

Lydia seated herself on the white couch. Her silk pantsuit was a startling slash of purple against the pale cushions. "What I mean to say—I know it sounds awful—is that Nina was something of a disappointment to me. We offered her so many opportunities. To study abroad, for instance. At a boarding school in Switzerland. Her sister Wendy went and benefited wonderfully. But Nina refused to go. She insisted on staying home. Then there were the other things. The boys she brought home. The ridiculous outfits she'd wear. She could be doing so much with her life, but she never achieved much."

"She earned a nursing degree."

Lydia gave a shrug. "So do thousands of other girls."

"She's not any other girl, Mrs. Warrenton. She's your daughter."

"That's why I expected more. Her sister speaks three languages and plays the piano and cello. She's married to an attorney who's in line for a judicial seat. While Nina..." Lydia sighed. "I can't imagine how sisters could be so different."

"Maybe the real difference," said Sam, rising to his feet, "was in how you loved them." He turned and walked out of the room.

"Mr. Navarro!" he heard Lydia call as he reached the front door.

He looked back. She was standing in the hallway, a woman of such perfectly groomed elegance that she didn't seem real or alive. Or touchable.

Not like Nina at all.

"I think you have entirely the wrong idea about me and my daughter," Lydia said.

"Does it really matter what I think?"

"I just want you to understand that I did the best I could, under the circumstances."

"Under the circumstances," replied Sam, "so did she." And he left the house.

Back in his car, he debated which way to head next. Another round of phone calls came up empty. Where the hell was she?

The only place he hadn't checked was her new apartment. She'd told him it was on Taylor Street. There was probably no phone in yet; he'd have to drive there to check it out.

On his way over, he kept thinking about what Lydia Warrenton had just told him. He thought about what it must have been like for Nina to grow up the black sheep, the un-favored child. Always doing the wrong thing, never meeting Mommy's approval. Sam had been fortunate to have a mother who'd instilled in him a sense of his own competence.

I understand now, he thought, *why you wanted to marry Robert.* Marrying Robert Bledsoe was the one sure way to gain her mother's approval. And even that had collapsed in failure.

By the time he pulled up at Nina's new apartment building, he was angry. At Lydia, at George Cormier and his parade of wives, at the entire Cormier family for its battering of a little girl's sense of self-worth.

He knocked harder at the apartment door than he had to.

There was no response. She wasn't here, either.

Where are you, Nina?

He was about to leave when he impulsively gave the knob a turn. It was unlocked.

He pushed the door open. "Nina?" he called.

Then his gaze focused on the wire. It was almost in-visible, a tiny line of silver that traced along the door-frame and threaded toward the ceiling.

Oh, my God...

In one fluid movement he pivoted away and dived sideways, down the hallway.

The force of the explosion blasted straight through the open door and ripped through the wall in a flying cloud of wood and plaster.

Deafened, stunned by the blast, Sam lay facedown in the hallway as debris rained onto his back.

Eight

"Man, oh man," said Gillis. "You sure did bring down the house."

They were standing outside, behind the yellow police line, waiting for the rest of the search team to assemble. The apartment house—what was left of it—had been cleared of any second devices, and now it was Ernie Takeda's show. Takeda was, at that moment, diagramming the search grid, handing out evidence bags, and assigning his lab crew to their individual tasks.

Sam already knew what they'd find. Residue of Dupont label dynamite. Scraps of green two-inch-wide electrical tape. And Prima detonating cord. The same three components as the church bomb and the warehouse bomb.

And every other bomb put together by the late Vincent Spectre.

Who's your heir apparent, Spectre? Sam wondered. *To whom did you bequeath your tricks of the trade? And why is Nina Cormier the target?*

Just trying to reason it through made his head pound.

He was still covered in dust, his cheek was bruised and swollen, and he could barely hear out of his left ear. But he had nothing to complain about. He was alive.

Nina would not have been so fortunate.

"I've got to find her," he said. "Before he does."

"We've checked with the family again," said Gillis. "Father, mother, sister. She hasn't turned up anywhere."

"Where the hell could she have gone?" Sam began to pace along the police line, his worry turning to agitation. "She walks out of headquarters, maybe she catches a cab or a bus. Then what? What would she do?"

"Whenever my wife gets mad, she goes shopping," Gillis offered helpfully.

"I'm going to call the family again." Sam turned to his car. "Maybe she's finally shown up somewhere."

He was about to reach inside the Taurus for the car phone when he froze, his gaze focused on the edge of the crowd. A small, dark-haired figure stood at the far end of the street. Even from that distance, Sam could read the fear, the shock, in her pale face.

"Nina," he murmured. At once he began to move toward her, began to push, then shove his way through the crowd. "Nina!"

She caught sight of him, struggling to reach her. Now she was moving as well, frantically plunging into the gathering of onlookers. They found each other, fell into each other's embrace. And at that moment, there was no one else in the world for Sam, no one but the woman he was holding. She felt so very precious in his arms, so easily taken from him.

With a sudden start, he became acutely aware of the crowd. All these people, pressing in on them. "I'm getting you out of here," he said. Hugging her close to his side, he guided her toward his car. The whole time, he was scanning faces, watching for any sudden movements.

Only when he'd bundled her safely into the Taurus did he allow himself a deep breath of relief.

"Gillis!" he called. "You're in charge here!"

"Where you going?"

"I'm taking her somewhere safe."

"But—"

Sam didn't finish the conversation. He steered the car out of the crowd and they drove away.

Drove north.

Nina was staring at him. At the bruise on his cheek, the plaster dust coating his hair. "My God, Sam," she murmured. "You've been hurt—"

"A little deaf in one ear, but otherwise I'm okay." He glanced at her and saw that she didn't quite believe him. "I ducked out just before it blew. It was a five-second delay detonator. Set off by opening the door." He paused, then added quietly, "It was meant for you."

She said nothing. She didn't have to; he could read the comprehension in her gaze. This bombing was no mistake, no random attack. She was the target and she could no longer deny it.

"We're chasing down every lead we have," he said. "Yeats is going to question Daniella again, but I think that's a dead end. We did get a partial fingerprint off the warehouse bomb, and we're waiting for an ID. Until then, we've just got to keep you alive. And that means you have to cooperate. Do exactly what I tell you to do." He gave an exasperated sigh and clutched the steering wheel tighter. "That was *not* smart, Nina. What you did today."

"I was angry. I needed to get away from all you cops."

"So you storm out of headquarters? Without telling me where you're going?"

"You threw me to the wolves, Sam. I expected Yeats to clap the handcuffs on me. And you delivered me to him."

"I had no choice. One way or the other, he was going to question you."

"Yeats thinks I'm guilty. And since *he* was so sure of it, I thought…I thought you must have your doubts as well."

"I have no doubts," he said, his voice absolutely steady. "Not about you. And after this latest bomb, I don't think Yeats'll have any doubts either. You're the target."

The turnoff to Route 95—the Interstate—was just ahead. Sam took it.

"Where are we going?" she asked.

"I'm getting you out of town. Portland isn't a safe place for you. So I have another spot in mind. A fishing camp on Coleman Pond. I've had it for a few years. You'll be roughing it there, but you can stay as long as you need to."

"You won't be staying with me?"

"I have a job to do, Nina. It's the only way we'll get the answers. If I do my job."

"Of course, you're right." And she looked straight ahead at the road. "I forget sometimes," she said softly, "that you're a cop."

ACROSS THE STREET from the police line, he stood in the thick of the crowd, watching the bomb investigators scurry about with their evidence bags and their notebooks. Judging by the shattered glass, the debris in the street, the blast had been quite impressive. But of course he'd planned it that way.

Too bad Nina Cormier was still alive.

He'd spotted her just moments before, being escorted through the crowd by Detective Sam Navarro. He'd recognized Navarro at once. For years he'd followed the man's career, had read every news article ever written about the Bomb Squad. He knew about Gordon Gillis and Ernie Takeda as well. It was his business to know. They were the enemy, and a good soldier must know his enemy.

Navarro helped the woman into a car. He seemed unusually protective—not like Navarro at all, to be succumbing to romance on the job. Cops like him were supposed to be professionals. What had happened to the quality of civil servants these days?

Navarro and the woman drove away.

There was no point trying to follow them; another opportunity would arise.

Right now he had a job to do. And only two days in which to finish it.

He gave his gloves a little tug. And he walked away, unnoticed, through the crowd.

BILLY "THE SHOWMAN" Binford was happy today. He was even grinning at his attorney, seated on the other side of the Plexiglas barrier.

"It's gonna be all right, Darien," said Billy. "I got everything taken care of. You just get ready to negotiate that plea bargain. And get me out of here, quick."

Darien shook his head. "I told you, Liddell's not in a mood to cut any deals. He's out to score big with your conviction."

"Darien, Darien. You got no faith."

"What I got is a good grip on reality. Liddell's aiming for a higher office. For that, he's got to put you away."

"He won't be putting anyone away. Not after Saturday."

"What?"

"You didn't hear me say nothing, okay? I didn't say nothing. Just believe me, Liddell won't be a problem."

"I don't want to know. Don't tell me about it."

Billy regarded his attorney with a look of both pity and amusement. "You know what? You're like that monkey with his paws over his ears. Hear no evil. That's you."

"Yeah," Darien agreed. And he nodded miserably. "That's me exactly."

A FIRE CRACKLED in the hearth, but Nina felt chilled to the bone. Outside, dusk had deepened, and the last light was fading behind the dense silhouettes of pine trees. The cry of a loon echoed, ghostlike, across the lake. She'd never been afraid of the woods, or the darkness, or of being alone. Tonight, though, she *was* afraid, and she didn't want Sam to leave.

She also knew he had to.

He came tramping back into the cottage, carrying an armload of firewood, and began to stack it by the hearth. "This should do you for a few days," he said. "I just spoke to Henry Pearl and his wife. Their camp's up the road. They said they'd check up on you a few times a day. I've known them for years, so I know you can count on them. If you need anything at all, just knock on their door."

He finished stacking the wood and clapped the dirt from his hands. With his shirtsleeves rolled up and sawdust clinging to his trousers, he looked more like a woodsman than a city cop. He threw another birch log on the fire and the flames shot up in a crackle of sparks. He turned to look at her, his expression hidden against the backlight of fire.

"You'll be safe here, Nina. I wouldn't leave you alone if I had even the slightest doubt."

She nodded. And smiled. "I'll be fine."

"There's a fishing pole and tackle box in the kitchen, if you feel like wrestling with a trout. And feel free to wear anything you find in the closet. None of it'll fit, but at least you'll be warm. Henry's wife'll drop by some, uh, women's wear tomorrow." He paused and laughed. "Those probably won't fit either. Since she's twice *my* size."

"I'll manage, Sam. Don't worry about me."

There was a long silence. They both knew there was nothing more to say, but he didn't move. He glanced around the room, as though reluctant to leave. Almost as reluctant as she was to see him go.

"It's a long drive back to the city," she said. "You should eat before you go. Can I interest you in dinner? Say, a gourmet repast of macaroni and cheese?"

He grinned. "Make it anything else and I'll say yes."

In the kitchen, they rummaged through the groceries they'd bought at a supermarket on the way. Mushroom omelets, a loaf of French bread, and a bottle of wine soon graced the tiny camp table. Electricity had not yet made it to this part of the lake, so they ate by the light of a hurricane lamp. Outside, dusk gave way to a darkness alive with the chirp of crickets.

She gazed across the table at him, watching the way his face gleamed in the lantern light. She kept focusing on that bruise on his cheek, thinking about how close he'd come to dying that afternoon. But that was exactly the sort of work he did, the sort of risk he took all the time. Bombs.

Death. It was insane, and she didn't know why any man in his right mind would take those risks. *Crazy cop,* she thought. *And I must be just as insane, because I think I'm falling for this guy.*

She took a sip of wine, the whole time intensely, almost painfully aware of his presence. And of her attraction toward him, an attraction so strong she was having trouble remembering to eat.

She had to remind herself that he was just doing his job, that to him, she was nothing more than a piece of the puzzle he was trying to solve, but she couldn't help picturing other meals, other nights they might spend together. Here, on the lake. Candlelight, laughter. Children. She thought he'd be good with children. He'd be patient and kind, just as he was with her.

How would I know that? I'm dreaming. Fantasizing again.

She reached across to pour him more wine.

He put his hand over the glass. "I have to be driving back."

"Oh. Of course." Nervously she set the bottle down again. She folded and refolded her napkin. For a whole minute they didn't speak, didn't look at each other. At least, she didn't look at him.

But when she finally raised her eyes, she saw that he was watching her. Not the way a cop looks at a witness, at a piece of a puzzle.

He was watching her the way a man watches a woman he wants.

He said, quickly, "I should leave now—"

"I know."

"—before it gets too late."

"It's still early."

"They'll need me, back in the city."

She bit her lip and said nothing. Of course he was right. The city did need him. Everyone needed him. She was just one detail that required attending to. Now she was safely tucked away and he could go back to his real business, his real concerns.

But he didn't seem at all eager to leave. He hadn't moved from the chair, hadn't broken eye contact. She was the one who looked away, who nervously snatched up her wineglass.

She was startled when he reached over and gently caught her hand. Without a word he took the glass and set it down. He raised her hand, palm side up, and pressed a kiss, ever so light, to her wrist. The lingering of lips, the tickle of his breath, was the sweetest torture. If he could wreak such havoc kissing that one square inch of skin, what could he do with the rest of her?

She closed her eyes and gave a small, soft moan. "I don't want you to leave," she whispered.

"It's a bad idea. For me to stay."

"Why?"

"Because of this." He kissed her wrist again. "And this." His lips skimmed up her arm, his beard delightfully rough against her sensitive skin. "It's a mistake. You know it. I know it."

"I make mistakes all the time," she replied. "I don't always regret them."

His gaze lifted to hers. He saw both her fear and her fearlessness. She was hiding nothing now, letting him read all. Her hunger was too powerful to hide.

He rose from the table. So did she.

He pulled her toward him, cupped her face in his hands, and pressed his lips to hers. The kiss, sweet with the taste of wine and desire, left her legs unsteady. She swayed against him, her arms reaching up to clutch his shoulders. Before she could catch her breath, he was kissing her again, deeper. As their mouths joined, so did their bodies. His hands slid down her waist, to her hips. He didn't need to pull her against him; she could already feel him, hard and aroused. And that excited her even more.

"If we're going to stop," he breathed, "it had better be now...."

She responded with a kiss that drowned out any more words between them. Their bodies did all the talking, all the communicating.

They were tugging at each other's clothes, feverish for the touch of bare skin. First her sweater came off, then his shirt. They kissed their way into the next room, where the fire had quieted to a warm glow. Still kissing her, he pulled the afghan off the couch and let it fall onto the floor by the hearth.

Facing each other, they knelt before the dying fire. His bare shoulders gleamed in the flickering light. She was eager, starved for his touch, but he moved slowly, savoring every moment, every new experience of her. He watched with longing as she unhooked her bra and shrugged the straps off her shoulders. When he reached out to cup her breast, to tug at her nipple, she let her head sag back with a moan. His touch was ever so gentle, yet it left her feeling weak. Conquered. He tipped her back and lowered her onto the afghan.

Her body was pure liquid now, melting under his touch. He unzipped her jeans, eased them off her hips. Her underwear slid off with the hiss of silk. She lay unshielded to his gaze now, her skin rosy in the firelight.

"I've had so many dreams about you," he whispered as

his hand slid exploringly down her belly, toward the dark triangle of hair. "Last night, when you were in my house, I dreamed of holding you. Touching you just the way I am now. But when I woke up, I told myself it could never happen. That it was all fantasy. All longing. And here we are..." He bent forward, his kiss tender on her lips. "I shouldn't be doing this."

"I want you to. I want us to."

"I want it just as much. More. But I'm afraid we're going to regret it."

"Then we'll regret it later. Tonight, let's just be you and me. Let's pretend there's nothing else, no one else."

He kissed her again. And this time his hand slipped between her thighs, his finger dipping into her wetness, sliding deep into her warmth. She groaned, helpless with delight. He slid another finger in, and felt her trembling, tightening around him. She was ready, so ready for him, but he wanted to take his time, to make this last.

He withdrew his hand, just long enough to remove the rest of his clothes. As he knelt beside her, she couldn't help drawing in a sharp breath of admiration. What a beautiful man he was. Not just his body, but his soul. She could see it in his eyes: the caring, the warmth. Before it had been hidden from her, concealed behind that tough-cop mask of his. Now he was hiding nothing. Revealing everything.

As she was revealing everything to him.

She was too lost in pleasure to feel any modesty, any shame. She lay back, whimpering, as his fingers found her again, withdrew, teased, plunged back in. Already she was slick with sweat and desire, her hips arching against him.

"Please," she murmured. "Oh, Sam. I—"

He kissed her, cutting off any protest. And he continued his torment, his fingers dipping, sliding, until she was wound so tight she thought she'd shatter.

Only then, only as she reached the very edge, did he take away his hand, fit his hips to hers, and thrust deep inside her.

She gripped him, crying out as he swept her, and himself, toward climax. And when it came, when she felt herself tumbling into that wondrous free fall, they clung to each other and they tumbled together, to a soft and ever-so-gentle landing.

She fell asleep, warm and safe, in his arms.

It was later, much later, when she awakened in the deepest chill of night.

The fire had died out. Although she was cocooned in the afghan, she found herself shivering.

And alone.

Hugging the afghan to her shoulders, she went into the kitchen and peered out the window. By the light of the moon, she could see that Sam's car was gone. He had returned to the city.

Already I miss him, she thought. Already his absence was like a deep, dark gulf in her life.

She went into the bedroom, climbed under the blankets, and tried to stop shivering, but she could not. When Sam had left, he had taken with him all the warmth. All the joy.

It scared her, how much she felt his absence. She was not going to fall in love with him; she could not afford to. What they'd experienced tonight was pleasure. The enjoyment of each other's bodies. As a lover, he was superb.

But as a man to love, he was clearly wrong for her.

No wonder he'd stolen away like a thief in the night. He'd known it was a mistake, just as she did. At this moment, he was probably regretting what they'd done.

She burrowed deeper under the blankets and waited for sleep, for dawn—whichever came first. Anything to ease the ache of Sam's departure.

But the night, cold and lonely, stretched on.

IT WAS A MISTAKE. A stupid, crazy mistake.

All the way back to Portland, on the drive down that long, dark highway, Sam kept asking himself how he could have let it happen.

No, he *knew* how it happened. The attraction between them was just too strong. It had been pulling them together from the first day they'd met. He'd fought it, had never stopped reminding himself that he was a cop, and she was an important element in his investigation. Good cops did not fall into this trap.

He used to think he was a good cop. Now he knew he was far too human, that Nina was a temptation he couldn't resist, and that the whole investigation would probably suffer because he'd lost his sense of objectivity.

All because she'd come to mean too much to him.

Not only would the investigation suffer, *he* would as well, and he had only himself to blame. Nina was scared and vulnerable; naturally she'd turn to her protector for comfort. He should have kept her at arm's length, should have kept his own urges in check. Instead he'd succumbed, and now she was all he could think about.

He gripped the steering wheel and forced himself to focus on the road. On the case.

By 1:00 a.m., he was back in the city. By 1:30, he was at his desk, catching up on the preliminary reports from Ernie Takeda. As he'd expected, the bomb in Nina's apartment was similar to the devices that blew up the church and the warehouse. The difference between the three was in the method of detonation. The warehouse device had had a simple timer. The church device was a package bomb, designed to explode on opening. Nina's apartment had been wired to blow after the door opened. This bomber was a versatile fellow. He could trigger a blast in any number of ways. He varied his device according to the situation, and that made him both clever and extremely dangerous.

He went home at 5:00 a.m., caught a few hours of sleep, and was back at headquarters for an eight o'clock meeting.

With three bombings in two weeks, the pressure was on, and the tension showed in the faces around the conference table. Gillis looked beat, Chief Coopersmith was testy, and even the normally unemotional Ernie Takeda was showing flashes of irritation. Part of that irritation was due to the presence of two federal agents from Alcohol, Tobacco and Firearms. Both the men from ATF wore expressions of big-time experts visiting Hicksville.

But the most annoying source of irritation was the presence of their esteemed D.A. and perpetual pain in the neck, Norm Liddell.

Liddell was waving the morning edition of the *New York Times*. "Look at the headline," he said. "'Portland, Maine, the new bombing capital?' New York's saying that about us? *Us?*" He threw the newspaper down on the table. "What the hell is going on in this town? Who *is* this bomber?"

"We can give you a likely psychological profile," said one of the ATF agents. "He's a white male, intelligent—"

"I already know he's intelligent!" snapped Liddell. "A hell of a lot more intelligent than we are. I don't want some psychological profile. I want to know who he *is*. Does anyone have any idea about his identity?"

There was a silence at the table. Then Sam said, "We know who he's trying to kill."

"You mean the Cormier woman?" Liddell snorted. "So far, no one's come up with a single good reason why she's the target."

"But we know she is. She's our one link to the bomber."

"What about the warehouse bomb?" said Coopersmith. "How's that connect to Nina Cormier?"

Sam paused. "That I don't know," he admitted.

"I'd lay ten-to-one odds that Billy Binford's people ordered that warehouse bombing," said Liddell. "It was a logical move on his part. Scare off a prosecution witness. Does the Cormier woman have any connection to Binford?"

"All she knows about him is what she's read in the newspapers," said Sam. "There's no link."

"What about her family? Are they linked at all to Binford?"

"No link there, either," spoke up Gillis. "We've checked into the finances of the whole family. Nina Cormier's father, mother, stepfather, stepmother. No connection to Binford. Her ex-fiancé was just as clean."

Liddell sat back. "Something's coming. I can feel it. Binford's got something big planned."

"How do you know?" asked Coopersmith.

"I have sources." Liddell shook his head in disgust. "Here I finally get The Snowman behind bars, and he's still pulling strings, still making mincemeat of the court system. I'm convinced that warehouse bomb was an intimidation tactic. He's trying to scare all my witnesses. If

I don't get a conviction, he'll be a free man in a few months. And he'll be scaring them in person."

"But chances are good you'll get that conviction," Coopersmith reassured him. "You've got credible witnesses, financial records. And you've drawn a law-and-order judge."

"Even so," countered Liddell, "Binford's not finished maneuvering. He's got something up his sleeve. I just wish I knew what it was." He looked at Sam. "Where are you hiding Nina Cormier?"

"A safe place," said Sam.

"You keeping it top secret or something?"

"Under the circumstances, I'd prefer to keep it known only to myself and Gillis. If you have questions to ask her, I can ask them for you."

"I just want to know what her connection is to these bombings. Why The Snowman wants her dead."

"Maybe this has nothing to do with Binford," suggested Sam. "He's in jail, and there's another party involved here. The bomber."

"Right. So find him for me," snapped Liddell. "Before Portland gets known as the American Beirut." He rose from his chair, his signal that the meeting was over. "Binford goes to trial in a month. I don't want my witnesses scared off by any more bombs. So *get* this guy, before he destroys my case." With that, Liddell stalked out.

"Man, election year is hell," muttered Gillis.

As the others filed out of the room, Coopersmith said, "Navarro, a word with you."

Sam waited, knowing full well what was coming. Coopersmith shut the door and turned to look at him.

"You and Nina Cormier. What's going on?"

"She needs protection. So I'm looking out for her."

"Is that all you're doing?"

Sam let out a weary sigh. "I...may be more involved than I should be."

"That's what I figured." Coopersmith shook his head. "You're too smart for this, Sam. This is the sort of mistake rookies make. Not you."

"I know."

"It could put you both in a dangerous situation. I ought to yank you off the case."

"I need to stay on it."

"Because of the woman?"

"Because I want to nail this guy. I'm *going* to nail him."

"Fine. Just keep your distance from Nina Cormier. I shouldn't have to tell you this. This kind of thing happens, someone always gets hurt. Right now she thinks you're John Wayne. But when this is all over, she's gonna see you're human like the rest of us. Don't set yourself up for this, Sam. She's got looks, she's got a daddy with lots of money. She doesn't want a cop."

I know he's right, thought Sam. *I know it from personal experience. Someone's going to get hurt. And it'll be me.*

The conference room door suddenly swung open and an excited Ernie Takeda stuck his head in the room. "You're not gonna believe this," he said, waving a sheet of fax paper.

"What is it?" asked Coopersmith.

"From NCIC. They just identified that fingerprint off the bomb fragment."

"And?"

"It's a match. With Vincent Spectre."

"That's impossible!" exclaimed Sam. He snatched the

sheet from Ernie's grasp and stared at the faxed report. What he read there left no doubt that the ID was definite.

"There has to be a mistake," said Coopersmith. "They found his body. Spectre's been dead and buried for months."

Sam looked up. "Obviously not," he growled.

Nine

The rowboat was old and well used, but the hull was sound. At least, it didn't leak as Nina rowed it out into the lake. It was late afternoon and a pair of loons were paddling lazily through the water, neither one alarmed by the presence of a lone rower. The day was utter stillness, utter peace, as warm as a summer day should be.

Nina guided the boat to the center of the pond, where sunlight rippled on the water, and there she let the boat drift. As it turned lazy circles, she lay back and stared up at the sky. She saw birds winging overhead, saw a dragonfly hover, iridescent in the slanting light.

And then she heard a voice, calling her name.

She sat up so sharply the boat rocked. She saw him then, standing at the water's edge, waving to her.

As she rowed the boat back to shore, her heart was galloping, more from anticipation than exertion. Why had he returned so soon? Last night he'd left without a word of goodbye, the way a man leaves a woman he never intends to see again.

Now here he was, standing silent and still on the shore, his gaze as unreadable as ever. She couldn't figure him out. She'd never be able to figure him out. He was a man designed to drive her crazy, and as she glided across the last yards of water, she could already feel that lovely insanity take hold of her. It required all her willpower to suppress it.

She tossed him the painter rope. He hauled the rowboat up onto the shore and helped her step out. Just the pressure of his hand grasping her arm gave her a thrill of delight. But one look at his face quelled any hopes that he was here as a lover. This was the cop, impersonal, businesslike. Not at all the man who'd held her in his arms.

"There's been a new development," he said.

Just as coolly, she met his gaze. "What development?"

"We think we know who the bomber is. I want you to take a look at some photographs."

On the couch by the fireplace—the same fireplace that had warmed them when they'd made love the night before—Nina sat flipping through a book of mug shots. The hearth was now cold, and so was she, both in body and in spirit. Sam sat a good foot away, not touching her, not saying a word. But he was watching her expectantly, waiting for some sign that she recognized a face in that book.

She forced herself to concentrate on the photos. One by one she scanned the faces, carefully taking in the features of each man pictured there. She reached the last page. Shaking her head, she closed the cover.

"I don't recognize anyone," she declared.

"Are you certain?"

"I'm certain. Why? Who am I supposed to recognize?"

His disappointment was apparent. He opened the book

to the fourth page and handed it back to her. "Look at this face. Third one down, first column. Have you ever seen this man?"

She spent a long time studying the photo. Then she said, "No. I don't know him."

With a sigh of frustration, Sam sank back against the couch. "This doesn't make any sense at all."

Nina was still focused on the photograph. The man in the picture appeared to be in his forties, with sandy hair, blue eyes, and hollow, almost gaunt, cheeks. It was the eyes that held her attention. They stared straight at her, a look of intimidation that burned, lifelike, from a mere two-dimensional image. Nina gave an involuntary shiver.

"Who is he?" she asked.

"His name is—or was—Vincent Spectre. He's five foot eleven, 180 pounds, forty-six years old. At least, that's what he would be now. If he's still alive."

"You mean you don't know if he is?"

"We thought he was dead."

"You're not sure?"

"Not any longer." Sam rose from the couch. It was getting chilly in the cabin; he crouched at the hearth and began to arrange kindling in the fireplace.

"For twelve years," he said, "Vincent Spectre was an army demolitions expert. Then he got booted out of the service. Dishonorable discharge, petty theft. It didn't take him long to launch a second career. He became what we call a specialist. Big bangs, big bucks. Hired himself out to anyone who'd pay for his expertise. He worked for terrorist governments. For the mob. For crime bosses all over the country.

"For years he raked in the money. Then his luck ran out.

He was recognized on a bank security camera. Arrested, convicted, served only a year. Then he escaped."

Sam struck a match and lit the kindling. It caught fire in a crackle of sparks and flames. He lay a log on top and turned to look at her.

"Six months ago," he continued, "Spectre's remains were found in the rubble after one of his bombs blew up a warehouse. That is, authorities *thought* it was his body. Now we think it might have been someone else's. And Spectre's still alive."

"How do you know that?"

"Because his fingerprint just turned up. On a fragment of the warehouse bomb."

She stared at him. "You think he also blew up the church?"

"Almost certainly. Vincent Spectre's trying to kill you."

"But I don't know any Vincent Spectre! I've never even heard his name before!"

"And you don't recognize his photo."

"No."

Sam stood up. Behind him, the flames were now crackling, consuming the log. "We've shown Spectre's photo to the rest of your family. They don't recognize him, either."

"It must be a mistake. Even if the man's alive, he has no reason to kill me."

"Someone else could have hired him."

"You've already explored that. And all you came up with was Daniella."

"That's still a possibility. She denies it, of course. And she passed the polygraph test."

"She let you hook her up to a *polygraph?*"

"She consented. So we did it."

Nina shook her head in amazement. "She must have been royally ticked off."

"As a matter of fact, I think she rather enjoyed giving the performance. She turned every male head in the department."

"Yes, she's good at that. She certainly turned my father's head. And Robert's, too," Nina added softly.

Sam was moving around the room now, pacing a slow circle around the couch. "So we're back to the question of Vincent Spectre," he said. "And what his connection is to you. Or Robert."

"I told you, I've never heard his name before. I don't remember Robert ever mentioning the name, either."

Sam paced around the couch, returned to stand by the fireplace. Against the background of flames, his face was unreadable. "Spectre *is* alive. And he built a bomb intended for you and Robert. Why?"

She looked down again at the photo of Vincent Spectre. Try as she might, she could conjure up no memory of that face. The eyes, perhaps, seemed vaguely familiar. That stare was one she might have seen before. But not the face.

"Tell me more about him," she suggested.

Sam went to the couch and sat down beside her. Not quite close enough to touch her, but close enough to make her very aware of his presence.

"Vincent Spectre was born and raised in California. Joined the army at age nineteen. Quickly showed an aptitude for explosives work, and was trained in demolitions. Saw action in Grenada and Panama. That's where he lost his finger—trying to disarm a terrorist explosive. At that point, he could have retired on disability but—"

"Wait. Did you just say he was missing a finger?"

"That's right."

"Which hand?"

"The left. Why?"

Nina went very still. Thinking, remembering. A missing finger. Why did that image seem so vividly familiar?

Softly she said, "Was it the left middle finger?"

Frowning, Sam reached for his briefcase and took out a file folder. He flipped through the papers contained inside. "Yes," he said. "It was the middle finger."

"No stump at all? Just...missing entirely."

"That's right. They had to amputate all the way back to the knuckle." He was watching her, his eyes alert, his voice quiet with tension. "So you *do* know him."

"I—I'm not sure. There was a man with an amputated finger—the left middle finger—"

"What? Where?"

"The Emergency Room. It was a few weeks ago. I remember he was wearing gloves, and he didn't want to take them off. But I had to check his pulse. So I pulled off the left glove. And I was so startled to see he was missing a finger. He'd stuffed the glove finger with cotton. I think I...I must have stared. I remember I asked him how he lost it. He told me he'd caught it in some machinery."

"Why was he in the ER?"

"It was—I think an accident. Oh, I remember. He was knocked down by a bicycle. He'd cut his arm and needed stitches put in. The strange part about it all was the way he vanished afterward. Right after the cut was sutured, I left the room to get something. When I came back, he was gone. No thank you, nothing. Just—disappeared. I thought he was trying to get away without paying his bill. But I found out later that he did pay the clerk. In cash."

"Do you remember his name?"

"No." She gave a shrug. "I'm terrible with names."

"Describe him for me. Everything you remember."

She was silent for a moment, struggling to conjure up the face of a man she'd seen weeks ago, and only once. "I remember he was fairly tall. When he lay down on the treatment table, his feet hung over the edge." She looked at Sam. "He'd be about your height."

"I'm six feet. Vincent Spectre's five-eleven. What about his face? Hair, eyes?"

"He had dark hair. Almost black. And his eyes..." She sat back, frowning in concentration. Remembered how startled she'd been by the missing finger. That she'd looked up and met the patient's gaze. "I think they were blue."

"The blue eyes would match Spectre's. The black hair doesn't. He could've dyed it."

"But the face was different. It didn't look like this photo."

"Spectre has resources. He could've paid for plastic surgery, completely changed his appearance. For six months we assumed he was dead. During that time he could've remade himself into an entirely different man."

"All right, what if it *was* Spectre I saw in the ER that day? Why does that make me a target? Why would he want to kill me?"

"You saw his face. You could identify him."

"A lot of people must have seen his face!"

"You're the only one who could connect that face with a man who was missing a finger. You said he was wearing gloves, that he didn't want to remove them."

"Yes, but it was part of his uniform. Maybe the only reason for the gloves was—"

"What uniform?"

"Some sort of long-sleeved jacket with brass buttons. White gloves. Pants with this side stripe. You know, like an elevator operator. Or a bellhop."

"Was there a logo embroidered on the jacket? A building or hotel name?"

"No."

Sam was on his feet now, pacing back and forth with new excitement. "Okay. Okay, he has a minor accident. Cuts his arm, has to go to the ER for stitches. You see that he's missing a finger. You see his face. And you see he's wearing some sort of uniform...."

"It's not enough to make me a threat."

"Maybe it is. Right now, he's operating under a completely new identity. The authorities have no idea what he looks like. But that missing finger is a giveaway. You saw it. And his face. You could identify him for us."

"I didn't know anything about Vincent Spectre. I wouldn't have thought to go to the police."

"We were already raising questions about his so-called death. Wondering if he was still alive and operating. Another bombing, and we might have figured out the truth. All we had to do was tell the public we were looking for a man missing his left middle finger. You would have come forward. Wouldn't you?"

She nodded. "Of course."

"That may be what he was afraid of. That you'd tell us the one thing we didn't know. What he looks like."

For a long moment she was silent. She was staring down at the book of mug shots, thinking about that day in the ER. Trying to remember the patients, the crises. Sore throats and sprained ankles. She'd been a nurse for eight years, had treated so many patients, that the days all seemed to blend together. But she did remember one more detail about that visit from the man with the gloves. A detail that left her suddenly chilled.

"The doctor," she said softly. "The doctor who sutured the cut—"

"Yes? Who was it?"

"Robert. It was Robert."

Sam stared at her. In that instant, he understood. They both did. Robert had been in the same room as well. He'd seen the patient's face, had seen the mutilated left hand. He, like Nina, could have identified Vincent Spectre.

Now Robert was dead.

Sam reached down to take Nina's hand. "Come on." He pulled her to her feet.

They were standing face-to-face now, and she felt her body respond immediately to his nearness, felt her stomach dance that little dance of excitement. Arousal.

"I'm driving you back to Portland," he said.

"Tonight?"

"I want you to meet with our police artist. See if you two can come up with a sketch of Spectre's face."

"I'm not sure I can. If I saw him, I'd recognize him. But just to describe his face—"

"The artist will walk you through it. The important thing is that we have something to work with. Also, I need you to help me go through the ER records. Maybe there's some information you've forgotten."

"We keep a copy of all the encounter forms. I can find his record for you." *I'll do anything you want me to do,* she thought, *if only you'll stop this tough-cop act.*

As they stood gazing at each other, she thought she saw a ripple of longing in his eyes. Too quickly, he turned away to get a jacket from the closet. He draped it over her shoulders. Just the brushing of his fingers against her skin made her quiver.

She shifted around to face him. To confront him.

"Has something happened between us?" she asked softly.

"What do you mean?"

"Last night. I didn't imagine it, Sam. We made love, right here in this room. Now I'm wondering what I did wrong. Why you seem so…indifferent."

He sighed, a sound of weariness. And perhaps regret. "Last night," he began, "shouldn't have happened. It was a mistake."

"I didn't think so."

"Nina, it's always a mistake to fall in love with the investigating cop. You're scared, you're looking for a hero. I happen to fall into the role."

"But you're not playing a role! Neither am I. Sam, I care about you. I think I'm falling in love with you."

He just looked at her without speaking, his silence as cutting as any words.

She turned away, so that she wouldn't have to see that flat, emotionless gaze of his. With a forced laugh she said, "God, I feel like such an idiot. Of course, this must happen to you all the time. Women throwing themselves at you."

"It's not like that."

"Isn't it? The hero cop. Who could resist?" She turned back to him. "So, how do I compare with all the others?"

"There aren't any others! Nina, I'm not trying to shove you away. I just want you to understand that it's the situation that's pulled us together. The danger. The intensity. You look at me and you completely miss all the flaws. All the reasons I'm not the right guy for you. You were engaged to Robert Bledsoe. Ivy League. Medical degree. House on the water. What the hell am I but a civil servant?"

She shook her head, tears suddenly filling her eyes. "Do you really think that's how I see you? As just a civil servant? Just a cop?"

"It's what I am."

"You're so much more." She reached up to touch his face. He flinched, but didn't pull away as her fingers caressed the roughness of his jaw. "Oh, Sam. You're kind. And gentle. And brave. I haven't met any other man like you. Okay, so you're a cop. It's just part of who you are. You've kept me alive. You've watched over me...."

"It was my job."

"Is that all it was?"

He didn't answer right away. He just looked at her, as though reluctant to tell the truth.

"Is it, Sam? Just a part of your job?"

He sighed. "No," he admitted. "It was more than that. You're more than that."

Pure joy made her smile. Last night she'd felt it—his warmth, his caring. For all his denials, there was a living, breathing man under that mask of indifference. She wanted so badly to fall into his arms, to coax the real Sam Navarro out from his hiding place.

He reached up for her hand and gently but firmly lowered it from his face. "Please, Nina," he said. "Don't make this hard for both of us. I have a job to do, and I can't be distracted. It's dangerous. For you and for me."

"But you do care. That's all I need to know. That you care."

He nodded. It was the most she could hope for.

"It's getting late. We should leave," he mumbled. And he turned toward the door. "I'll be waiting for you in the car."

NINA FROWNED at the computer-generated sketch of the suspect's face. "It's not quite right," she said.

"What's not right about it?" asked Sam.

"I don't know. It's not easy to conjure up a man's face. I saw him only that one time. I didn't consciously register the shape of his nose or jaw."

"Does he look anything like this picture?"

She studied the image on the computer screen. For an hour, they'd played with different hairlines, noses, shapes of jaws and chins. What they'd come up with seemed generic, lifeless. Like every other police sketch she'd ever seen.

"To be honest," she admitted with a sigh, "I can't be sure this is what he looks like. If you put the real man in a lineup, I think I'd be able to identify him. But I'm not very good at re-creating what I saw."

Sam, obviously disappointed, turned to the computer technician. "Print it up anyway. Send copies to the news stations and wire services."

"Sure thing, Navarro," the tech replied and he flipped on the printer switch.

As Sam led Nina away, she said miserably, "I'm sorry. I guess I wasn't much help."

"You did fine. And you're right, it's not easy to re-create a face. Especially one you saw only once. You really think you'd know him if you saw him?"

"Yes. I'm pretty sure of it."

He gave her arm a squeeze. "That may be all we'll need from you. Assuming we ever get our hands on him. Which leads to the next item on our agenda."

"What's that?"

"Gillis is already at the hospital, pulling those treatment records. He'll need you to interpret a few things on the encounter form."

She nodded. "*That* I know I can do."

They found Gillis sitting in a back room of the ER, papers piled up on the table in front of him. His face was pasty with fatigue under the fluorescent lights. It was nearly midnight, and he'd been on the job since 7:00 a.m. So had Sam.

For both of them, the night was just beginning.

"I pulled what I think is the right encounter form," said Gillis. "May 29, 5:00 p.m. Sound about right, Miss Cormier?"

"It could be."

Gillis handed her the sheet. It was the one-page record of an ER visit. On top was the name Lawrence Foley, his address, and billing information. On the line Chief Complaint, she recognized her own handwriting: Laceration, left forearm. Below that, she had written: forty-six-year-old white male hit by bicycle in crosswalk. Fell, cut arm on fender. No loss of consciousness."

She nodded. "This is the one. Here's Robert's signature, on the bottom. Treating physician. He sutured the cut— four stitches, according to his notes."

"Have we checked out this name, Lawrence Foley?" Sam asked Gillis.

"No one by that name living at that address," Gillis informed him. "And that's a nonexistent phone number."

"Bingo," said Sam. "False address, false identity. This is our man."

"But we're no closer to catching him," stressed Gillis.

"He left no trail, no clues. Where are we supposed to look?"

"We have a sketch of his face circulating. We know he was wearing some sort of uniform, possibly a bellhop's. So we check all the hotels. Try to match the sketch with any of their employees." Sam paused, frowning. "A hotel. Why would he be working at a hotel?"

"He needed a job?" Gillis offered.

"As a bellhop?" Sam shook his head. "If this is really Vincent Spectre, he had a reason to be there. A contract. A target…" He sat back and rubbed his eyes. The late hour, the stress, was showing in his face. All those shadows, all those lines of weariness. Nina longed to reach out to him, to stroke away the worry she saw there, but she didn't dare. Not in front of Gillis. Maybe not ever. He'd made it perfectly clear she was a distraction to him, to his work, and that distractions were dangerous. That much she accepted.

Yet how she ached to touch him.

Sam rose to his feet and began to move about, as though forcing himself to stay awake. "We need to check all the hotels. Set up a lineup of bellhops. And we need to check police reports. Maybe someone called in that bicycle accident."

"Okay, I'll get Cooley on it."

"What we really need to know is—who is he after? Who's the target?"

"We're not going to figure that out tonight," said Gillis. "We need more to go on." He yawned, and added, "And we need some sleep. Both of us."

"He's right," said Nina. "You can't function without rest, Sam. You need to sleep on this."

"In the meantime, Spectre's at work on God knows what catastrophe. So far we've been lucky. Only one bombing casualty. But the next time..." Sam stopped pacing. Stopped because he'd simply run out of steam. He was standing in one spot, his shoulders slumped, his whole body drooping.

Gillis looked at Nina. "Get him home, will ya? Before he keels over and I have to drag him."

Nina rose from her chair. "Come on, Sam," she said softly. "I'll drive you home."

Heading out to the car, he kept insisting he could drive, that he was in perfectly good shape to take the wheel. She, just as insistently, pointed out that he was a menace on the road.

He let her drive.

Scarcely after she'd pulled out of the hospital parking lot, he was sound asleep.

At his house, she roused him just long enough to climb out of the car and walk in the front door. In his bedroom, he shrugged off his gun holster, pulled off his shoes, and collapsed on the bed. His last words were some sort of apology. Then he was fast asleep.

Smiling, she pulled the covers over him and went out to check the windows and doors. Everything was locked tight; the house was secure—as secure as it could be.

Back in Sam's room, she undressed in the dark and climbed into bed beside him. He didn't stir. Gently she stroked her fingers through his hair and thought, *My poor, exhausted Sam. Tonight, I'll watch over you.*

Sighing, he turned toward her, his arm reaching out to hug her against him. Even in his sleep, he was trying to protect her.

Like no other man I've ever known.
Nothing could hurt her. Not tonight, not in his arms.
She'd stake her life on it.

THEY WERE SHOWING his picture on the morning news.

Vincent Spectre took one look at the police sketch on the TV screen and he laughed softly. What a joke. The picture looked nothing like him. The ears were too big, the jaw was too wide, and the eyes looked beady. He did not have beady eyes. How had they gotten it so wrong? What had happened to the quality of law enforcement?

"Can't catch me, I'm the gingerbread man," he murmured.

Sam Navarro was slipping, if that drawing was the best he could come up with. A pity. Navarro had seemed such a clever man, a truly worthy opponent. Now it appeared he was as dumb a cop as all the others. Though he *had* managed to draw one correct conclusion.

Vincent Spectre was alive and back in the game.

"Just wait till you see how alive I am," he said.

That Cormier woman must have described his face to the police artist. Although the sketch wasn't anything for him to worry about, Nina Cormier did concern him. Chances were, she'd recognize him in a room of anonymous strangers. She was the only one who could link his face to his identity, the only one who could ruin his plan. She would have to be disposed of.

Eventually.

He turned off the TV and went into the apartment bedroom, where the woman was still asleep. He'd met Marilyn Dukoff three weeks ago at the Stop Light Club, where he'd gone to watch the topless dance revue. Marilyn had been the blonde in the purple-sequined G-string. Her face was coarse, her IQ a joke, but her figure was a marvel of nature and silicone. Like so many other women on the exotic dance circuit, she was in desperate need of money and affection.

He'd offered her both, in abundance.

She'd accepted his gifts with true gratitude. She was like a puppy who'd been neglected too long, loyal and hungry for approval. Best of all, she asked no questions. She knew enough not to.

He sat down beside her on the bed and nudged her awake. "Marilyn?"

She opened one sleepy eye and smiled at him. "Good morning."

He returned her smile. And followed it with a kiss. As usual, she responded eagerly. Gratefully. He removed his clothes and climbed under the sheets, next to that architecturally astonishing body. It took no coaxing at all to get her into the mood.

When they had finished, and she lay smiling and satisfied beside him, he knew it was the right time to ask.

And he said, "I need another favor from you."

TWO HOURS LATER, a blond woman in a gray suit presented her ID to the prison official. "I'm an attorney with Frick and Darien," she said. "Here to see our client, Billy Binford."

Moments later she was escorted to the visiting room. Billy "The Snowman" took a seat on the other side of the Plexiglas. He regarded her for a moment, then said, "I been watching the news on TV. What the hell's all this other stuff going on?"

"He says it's all necessary," said the blonde.

"Look, I just wanted the job done like he promised."

"It's being taken care of. Everything's on schedule. All you have to do is sit back and wait."

Billy glanced at the prison guard, who was standing off to the side and obviously bored. "I got everything riding on this," he muttered.

"It will happen. But he wants to make sure you keep up your end of the bargain. Payment, by the end of the week."

"Not yet. Not till I'm sure it's done. I got a court date coming up fast—too fast. I'm counting on this."

The blonde merely smiled. "It'll happen," she said. "He guarantees it."

Ten

Sam woke up to the smell of coffee and the aroma of something cooking, something delicious. It was Saturday. He was alone in the bed, but there was no question that someone else was in the house. He could hear the bustle in the kitchen, the soft clink of dishes. For the first time in months, he found himself smiling as he rose from bed and headed to the shower. There was a woman in the kitchen, a woman who was actually cooking breakfast. Amazing how different that made the whole house feel. Warm. Welcoming.

He came out of the shower and stood in front of the mirror to shave. That's when his smile faded. He suddenly wondered how long he'd been asleep. He'd slept so heavily he hadn't heard Nina get out of bed this morning, hadn't even heard her take a shower. But she'd been in here; the shower curtain had already been damp when he stepped in.

Last night someone could have broken into the house, and he would have slept right through it.

I'm useless to her, he thought. He couldn't track down

Spectre and keep Nina safe at the same time. He didn't have the stamina or the objectivity. He was worse than useless; he was endangering her life.

This was exactly what he'd been afraid would happen.

He finished shaving, got dressed, and went into the kitchen.

Just the sight of her standing at the stove was enough to shake his determination. She turned and smiled at him.

"Good morning," she murmured, and wrapped her arms around him in a sweetly scented hug. Lord, this was every man's fantasy. Or, at least, it was *his* fantasy: a gorgeous woman in his kitchen. The good morning smile. Pancakes cooking in the skillet.

A woman in the house.

Not just any woman. Nina. Already he felt his resistance weakening, felt the masculine urges taking over again. This was what always happened when he got too close to her.

He took her by the shoulders and stepped away. "Nina, we have to talk."

"You mean…about the case?"

"No. I mean about you. And me."

All at once that radiant smile was gone from her face. She'd sensed that a blow was about to fall, a blow that would be delivered by *him*. Mutely she turned, lifted the pancake from the skillet, and slid it onto a plate. Then she just stood there, looking at it lying on the countertop.

He hated himself at that moment. At the same time he knew there was no other way to handle this—not if he really cared about her.

"Last night shouldn't have happened," he said.

"But nothing *did* happen between us. I just brought you home and put you to bed."

"That's exactly what I'm talking about. Nina, I was so exhausted last night, someone could've driven a damn train through my bedroom and I wouldn't have moved a muscle. How am I supposed to keep you safe when I can't even keep my eyes open?"

"Oh, Sam." She stepped toward him, her hands rising to caress his face. "I don't expect you to be my guardian. Last night, I wanted to take care of *you*. I was so happy to do it."

"I'm the cop, Nina. I'm responsible for your safety."

"For once, can't you stop being a cop? Can't you let me take care of *you?* I'm not so helpless. And you're not so tough that you don't need someone. When I was scared, you were there for me. And I want to be here for *you*."

"I'm not the one who could get killed." He took both her hands and firmly lowered them from his face. "This isn't a good idea, getting involved, and we both know it. I can't watch out for you the way I should. Any other cop could do a better job."

"I don't trust any other cop. I trust you."

"And that could be a fatal mistake." He pulled away, gaining himself some breathing space. Anything to put distance between them. He couldn't think clearly when she was so near; her scent, her touch, were too distracting. He turned and matter-of-factly poured himself a cup of coffee, noting as he did it that his hand wasn't quite steady. Her effect, again. Not looking at her, he said, "It's time to focus on the case, Nina. On finding Spectre. That's the best way to ensure your safety. By doing my job and doing it right."

She said nothing.

He turned and saw that she was gazing listlessly at the table. It had already been set with silverware and napkins, glasses of juice, and a small crock of maple syrup. Again he felt that stab of regret. *I've finally found a woman I care about, a woman I could love, and I'm doing my best to push her away.*

"So," she said softly. "What do you propose, Sam?"

"I think another man should be assigned to protect you. Someone who has no personal involvement with you."

"Is that what we have? A personal involvement?"

"What else would you call it?"

She shook her head. "I'm beginning to think we have no involvement at all."

"For God's sake, Nina. We slept with each other! How can two people get more involved than that?"

"For some people, sex is purely a physical act. And that's all it is." Her chin tilted up in silent inquiry. *For some people.*

Meaning me?

Damn it, he refused to get caught up in this hopeless conversation. She was baiting him, trying to get him to admit there was more to that act of lovemaking than just sex. He was not about to admit the truth, not about to let her know how terrified he was of losing her.

He knew what had to be done.

He crossed the kitchen to the telephone. He'd call Coopersmith, ask him to assign a man to pull guard duty. He was about to pick up the receiver when the phone suddenly rang.

He answered it with a curt "Navarro."

"Sam, it's me."

"Morning, Gillis."

"Morning? It's nearly noon. I've already put in a full day here."

"Yeah, I'm hanging my head in shame."

"You should. We've got that lineup scheduled for one o'clock. Bellhops from five different hotels. You think you can bring Nina Cormier down here to take a look? That is, if she's there with you."

"She's here," admitted Sam.

"That's what I figured. Be here at one o'clock, got it?"

"We'll be there." He hung up and ran his hand through his damp hair. God. Nearly noon? He was getting lazy. Careless. All this agonizing over him and Nina, over a relationship that really had nowhere to go, was cutting into his effectiveness as a cop. If he didn't do his job right, *she* was the one who'd suffer.

"What did Gillis say?" he heard her ask.

He turned to her. "They've scheduled a lineup at one o'clock. Want you to look at a few hotel bellhops. You up to it?"

"Of course. I want this over with as much as you do."

"Good."

"And you're right about turning me over to another cop. It's all for the best." She met his gaze with a look of clear-eyed determination. "You have more important things to do than baby-sit me."

He didn't try to argue with her. In fact, he didn't say a thing. But as she walked out of the kitchen, leaving him standing alone by that cozily set breakfast table, he thought, *You're wrong. There's no more important job in the world to me than watching over you.*

EIGHT MEN STOOD on the other side of the one-way mirror. All of them were facing forward. All of them looked a little sheepish about being there.

Nina carefully regarded each man's uniform in turn, searching for any hint of familiarity. Any detail at all that might trip a memory.

She shook her head. "I don't see the right uniform."

"You're absolutely certain?" asked Gillis.

"I'm certain. It wasn't any of those."

She heard an undisguised snort of disappointment. It came from Norm Liddell, the D.A. who was standing next to Gillis. Sam, poker-faced, said nothing.

"Well, this was a big waste of my time," muttered Liddell. "Is this all you've come up with, Navarro? A bellhop roundup?"

"We know Spectre was wearing some sort of uniform similar to a bellhop's," said Sam. "We just wanted her to look over a few."

"We did track down a police report of that bike accident," said Gillis. "The bicyclist himself called it in. I think he was worried about a lawsuit, so he made a point of stating that he hit the man outside a crosswalk. Apparently, Spectre was jaywalking when he was hit on Congress Street."

"Congress?" Liddell frowned.

"Right near the Pioneer Hotel," said Sam. "Which, we've found out, is where the Governor plans to stay day after tomorrow. He's the guest speaker at some small business seminar."

"You think Spectre's target is the Governor?"

"It's a possibility. We're having the Pioneer checked and double-checked. Especially the Governor's room."

"What about the Pioneer's bellhops?"

"We eliminated all of them, just based on height and age. No one's missing any fingers. That one there— number three—is the closest to Spectre's description. But he has all his fingers, too. We just wanted Nina to take a look at the uniform, see if it jogged a memory."

"But no one in that lineup is Spectre."

"No. We've looked at everyone's hands. No missing fingers."

Nina's gaze turned to number three in the lineup. He was dressed in a bellhop's red jacket and black pants. "Is that what all the Pioneer's bellhops wear?" she asked.

"Yeah," said Gillis. "Why?"

"I don't think that's the uniform I saw."

"What's different about it?"

"The man I saw in the ER—I'm just remembering it— his jacket was green. Sort of a forest green. It was definitely not red."

Gillis shook his head. "We got us a problem then. The Holiday Inn's uniform is red, too. Marriott's green, but it's not located anywhere near the bicycle accident."

"Check out their staff anyway," Liddell ordered. "If you have to interview every bellhop in town, I want this guy caught. And I sure as hell want him caught before he blows up some high-muck-a-muck. When's the Governor arriving tomorrow?"

"Sometime in the afternoon," said Gillis.

Liddell glanced at his watch. "We have a full twenty-four hours. If anything comes up, I get called. Got it?"

"Yes, sir, your highness," muttered Gillis.

Liddell glanced sharply at him, but obviously decided to drop it. "My wife and I'll be at the Brant Theater tonight. I'll have my beeper with me, just in case."

"You'll be first on our list to call," said Sam.

"We're in the spotlight on this. So let's not screw up." It was Liddell's parting shot, and the two cops took it in silence.

Only after Liddell had left the room did Gillis growl, "I'm gonna get that guy. I swear, I'm gonna get him."

"Cool it, Gillis. He may be governor someday."

"In which case, I'll help Spectre plant the damn bomb myself."

Sam took Nina's arm and walked her out of the room. "Come on. I have my hands full today. I'll introduce you to your new watchdog."

Passing me off already, she thought. Was she such a nuisance to him?

"For now, we're keeping you in a hotel," he said. "Officer Pressler's been assigned to watch over you. He's a sharp cop. I trust him."

"Meaning I should, too?"

"Absolutely. I'll call you if we turn up any suspects. We'll need you to identify them."

"So I may not be seeing you for a while."

He stopped in the hallway and looked at her. "No. It may be a while."

They faced each other for a moment. The hallway was hardly private; certainly this wasn't the time or the place to confess how she felt about him. *She* wasn't even sure how she felt about him. All she knew was that it hurt to say goodbye. What hurt even worse was to look in his eyes and see no regret, no distress. Just that flat, unemotional gaze.

So it was back to Mr. Civil Servant. She could deal with that. After the trauma of this last week, she could deal with anything, including the realization that she had, once again, gotten involved with the wrong man.

She met his gaze with one just as cool and said, "You find Spectre. I'll identify him. Just do it soon, okay? So I can get on with my life."

"We're working on it round the clock. We'll keep you informed."

"Can I count on that?"

He answered with a curt dip of the head. "It's part of my job."

OFFICER LEON PRESSLER was not a conversationalist. In fact, whether he could converse at all was in question. For the past three hours, the muscular young cop had done a terrific sphinx imitation, saying nary a word as he roamed the hotel room, alternately checking the door and glancing out the third floor window. The most he would say was "Yes, ma'am," or "No, ma'am," and that was only in response to a direct question. Was the strong, silent bit some kind of cop thing? Nina wondered. Or was he under orders not to get too chatty with the witness?

She tried to read a novel she'd picked up in the hotel gift shop, but after a few chapters she gave up. His silence made her too nervous. It was simply not natural to spend a day in a hotel room with another person and not, at the very least, talk to each other. Lord knew, she tried to draw him out.

"Have you been a cop a long time, Leon?" she asked.

"Yes, ma'am."

"Do you enjoy it?"

"Yes, ma'am."

"Does it ever scare you?"

"No, ma'am."

"Never?"

"Sometimes."

Now they were getting somewhere, she thought.

But then Officer Pressler crossed the room and peered out the window, ignoring her.

She put her book aside and launched another attempt at conversation.

"Does this sort of assignment bore you?" she asked.

"No, ma'am."

"It would bore me. Spending all day in a hotel room doing nothing."

"Things could happen."

"And I'm sure you'll be ready for it." Sighing, she reached for the remote and clicked on the TV. Five minutes of channel surfing turned up nothing of interest. She clicked it off again. "Can I make a phone call?" she asked.

"Sorry."

"I just want to call my nursing supervisor at Maine Medical. To tell her I won't be coming in next week."

"Detective Navarro said no phone calls. It's necessary for your safety. He was very specific on that."

"What else did the good detective tell you?"

"I'm to keep a close eye. Not let my guard down for a minute. Because if anything happened to you…" He paused and gave a nervous cough.

"What?"

"He'd, uh, have my hide."

"That's quite an incentive."

"He wanted to make sure I took special care. Not that I'd let anything happen. I owe him that much."

She frowned at him. He was at the window again, peering down at the street. "What do you mean, you owe him?"

Officer Pressler didn't move from the window. He stood looking out, as though unwilling to meet her gaze. "It was a few years back. I was on this domestic call. Husband didn't much like me sticking my nose into his business. So he shot me."

"My god."

"I radioed for help. Navarro was first to respond." Pressler turned and looked at her. "So you see, I do owe him." Calmly he turned back to the window.

"How well do you know him?" she asked softly.

Pressler shrugged. "He's a good cop. But real private. I'm not sure anyone knows him very well."

Including me, she thought. Sighing, she clicked on the boob tube again and channel surfed past a jumble of daytime soaps, a TV court show and a golf tournament. She could almost feel another few brain cells collapse into mush.

What was Sam doing right now? she wondered.

And ruthlessly suppressed the thought. Sam Navarro was his own man. That much was perfectly clear.

She would have to be her own woman.

I WONDER WHAT Nina's doing right now. At once Sam tried to suppress the thought, tried to concentrate instead on what was being said at the meeting, but his mind kept drifting back to the subject of Nina. Specifically, her safety. He had every reason to trust Leon Pressler. The young cop was sharp and reliable, and he owed his life to Sam. If anyone could be trusted to keep Nina out of harm's way, it would be Pressler.

Still, he couldn't shake that lingering sense of uneasiness. And fear. It was one more indication that he'd lost his objectivity, that his feelings were way out of control. To the point of affecting his work...

"...the best we can do? Sam?"

Sam suddenly focused on Abe Coopersmith. "Excuse me?"

Coopersmith sighed. "Where the hell are you, Navarro?"

"I'm sorry. I let my attention drift for a moment."

Gillis said, "Chief asked if we're following any other leads."

"We're following every lead we have," Sam informed him. "The sketch of Spectre is circulating. We've checked all the hotels in Portland. So far, no employees with a missing finger. Problem is, we're operating blind. We don't know Spectre's target, when he plans to strike, or where he plans to strike. All we have is a witness who's seen his face."

"And this bit about the bellhop's uniform."

"That's right."

"Have you shown all those uniforms to Miss Cormier? To help us identify which hotel we're talking about?"

"We're getting together a few more samples for her to look at," said Gillis. "Also, we've interviewed that bicyclist. He doesn't remember much about the man he hit. It happened so fast, he didn't really pay attention to the face. But he does back up Miss Cormier's recollection that the uniform jacket was green. Some shade of it, anyway. And he confirms that it happened on Congress Street, near Franklin Avenue."

"We've combed that whole area," said Sam. "Showed the sketch to every shopkeeper and clerk within a five-block radius. No one recognized the face."

Coopersmith gave a grunt of frustration. "We've got the Governor arriving tomorrow afternoon. And a bomber somewhere in the city."

"We don't know if there's a connection. Spectre could be targeting someone else entirely. It all depends on who hired him."

"He may not even plan a hit at all," suggested Gillis. "Maybe he's finished his job. Maybe he's left town."

"We have to assume he's still here," cautioned Cooper-smith. "And up to no good."

Sam nodded in agreement. "We have twenty-four hours before the Governor's meeting. By then, something's bound to turn up."

"God, I hope so," said Coopersmith, and he rose to leave. "If there's one thing we don't need, it's another bomb going off. And a dead Governor."

"LET'S TAKE IT from the top. Measure 36." The conductor raised his baton, brought it down again. Four beats later, the trumpets blared out the opening notes of "Wrong Side of the Track Blues," to be joined seconds later by wood-winds and bass. Then the sax slid in, its plaintive whine picking up the melody.

"Never did understand jazz," complained the Brant Theater manager, watching the rehearsal from the middle aisle. "Lotta sour notes if you ask me. All the instruments fighting with each other."

"I like jazz," said the head usher.

"Yeah, well, you like rap, too. So I don't think much of your taste." The manager glanced around the theater, sur-veying the empty seats. He noted that everything was clean, that there was no litter in the aisles. The audience tonight would be a discriminating crowd. Bunch of lawyer types. They wouldn't appreciate sticky floors or wadded up programs in the chairs.

Just a year ago, this building had been a porn palace, showing X-rated films to an audience of nameless, faceless men. The new owner had changed all that. Now, with a little private money from a local benefactor, the Brant Theater had been rehabilitated into a live performance center, featuring stage plays and musical artists. Unfortunately, the live performances brought in fewer crowds than the porn had. The manager wasn't surprised.

Tonight, at least, a big audience was assured—five hundred paid and reserved seats, with additional walk-ins expected, to benefit the local Legal Aid office. Imagine that. All those lawyers actually paying to hear jazz. He didn't get it. But he was glad these seats would be filled.

"Looks like we may be short a man tonight," said the head usher.

"Who?"

"That new guy you hired. You know, the one from the Agency. Showed up for work two days ago. Haven't heard from him since. I tried calling him, but no luck."

The manager cursed. "Can't rely on these agency hires."

"That's for sure."

"You just gotta work the crowd with four men tonight."

"Gonna be a bear. Five hundred reserved seats and all."

"Let some of 'em find their own seats. They're lawyers. They're supposed to have brains." The manager glanced at his watch. It was six-thirty. He'd have just enough time to wolf down that corned beef sandwich in his office. "Doors open in an hour," he said. "Better get your supper now."

"Sure thing," replied the head usher. He swept up the green uniform jacket from the seat where he'd left it. And, whistling, he headed up the aisle for his dinner.

AT SEVEN-THIRTY, Officer Pressler escorted Nina back to police headquarters. The building was quieter than it had been that afternoon, most of the desks deserted, and only an occasional clerk circulating in the halls. Pressler brought Nina upstairs and ushered her into an office.

Sam was there.

He gave her only the most noncommittal of greetings: a nod, a quiet hello. She responded in kind. Pressler was in the room too, as were Gillis and another man in plainclothes, no doubt a cop as well. With an audience watching, she was not about to let her feelings show. Obviously Sam wasn't, either.

"We wanted you to take a look at these uniforms," Sam said, gesturing to the long conference table. Laid out on the table were a half dozen uniform jackets of various colors. "We've got bellhops, an elevator operator, and an usher's uniform from the downtown Cineplex. Do any of them strike you as familiar?"

Nina approached the table. Thoughtfully she eyed each one, examining the fabrics, the buttons. Some of them had embroidered hotel logos. Some were trimmed with gold braid or nametags.

She shook her head. "It wasn't one of these."

"What about that green one, on the end?"

"It has gold braid. The jacket I remember had black braid, sort of coiled up here, on the shoulder."

"Geez," murmured Gillis. "Women remember the weirdest things."

"Okay," Sam said with a sigh. "That's it for this session. Thanks, everyone. Pressler, why don't you take a break and get some supper. I'll bring Miss Cormier back to her hotel. You can meet us there in an hour or so."

The room emptied out. All except Sam and Nina.

For a moment, they didn't speak to each other. They didn't even look at each other. Nina almost wished that the earnest Officer Pressler was back with her again; at least *he* didn't make her feel like turning tail and running.

"I hope your hotel room's all right," he finally said.

"It's fine. But I'll be going stir crazy in another day. I have to get out of there."

"It's not safe yet."

"When will it be safe?"

"When we have Spectre."

"That could be never." She shook her head. "I can't live this way. I have a job. I have a life. I can't stay in a hotel room with some cop who drives me up a wall."

Sam frowned. "What's Pressler done?"

"He won't sit still! He never stops checking the windows. He won't let me touch the phone. And he can't carry on a decent conversation."

"Oh." Sam's frown evaporated. "That's just Leon doing his job. He's good."

"Maybe he is. But he still drives me crazy." Sighing, she took a step toward him. "Sam, I can't stay cooped up. I have to get on with my life."

"You will. But we have to get you through this part alive."

"What if I left town? Went somewhere else for a while—"

"We might need you here, Nina."

"You don't. You have his prints. You know he's missing a finger. You could identify him without any question—"

"But we need to spot him first. And for that, we might need you to pick him out of a crowd. So you have to stay in town. Available. We'll keep you safe, I promise."

"I suppose you'll have to. If you want to catch your man."

He took her by the shoulders. "That's not the only reason, and you know it."

"Do I?"

He leaned closer. For one astonishing moment she thought he was going to kiss her. Then a rap on the door made them both jerk apart.

Gillis, looking distinctly ill at ease, stood in the doorway. "Uh...I'm heading over to get a burger. You want I should get you something, Sam?"

"No. We'll pick something up at her hotel."

"Okay." Gillis gave an apologetic wave. "I'll be back here in an hour." He departed, leaving Sam and Nina alone once again.

But the moment was gone forever. If he'd intended to kiss her, she saw no hint of it in his face.

He said, simply, "I'll drive you back now."

In Sam's car, she felt as if they'd reverted right back to the very first day they'd met, to the time when he'd been the stone-faced detective and she'd been the bewildered citizen. It was as if all the events of the past week—their nights together, their lovemaking—had never happened. He seemed determined to avoid any talk of feelings tonight, and she was just as determined not to broach the subject.

The only safe topic was the case. And even on that topic, he was not very forthcoming.

"I notice you've circulated the police sketch," she said.

"It's been everywhere. TV, the papers."

"Any response?"

"We've been inundated by calls. We've spent all day chasing them down. So far, nothing's panned out."

"I'm afraid my description wasn't very helpful."

"You did the best you could."

She looked out the window, at the streets of downtown

Portland. It was already eight o'clock, the summer dusk
just slipping into night. "If I saw him again, I'd know him.
I'm sure I would."

"That's all we need from you, Nina."

All you want from me, too, she thought sadly. She asked,
"What happens tomorrow?"

"More of the same. Chase down leads. Hope someone
recognizes that sketch."

"Do you know if Spectre's even in the city?"

"No. He may be long gone. In which case we're just
spinning our wheels. But my instincts are telling me he's
still here somewhere. And he's got something planned,
something big." He glanced at her. "*You* could be the
wrench in the works. The one person who can recognize
him. That's why we have to keep you under wraps."

"I can't stand much more of this. I'm not even allowed
to make a phone call."

"We don't want people to know your whereabouts."

"I won't tell anyone. I promise. It's just that I feel so
cut off from everyone."

"Okay." He sighed. "Who do you want to call?"

"I could start with my sister, Wendy."

"I thought you two didn't get along."

"We don't. But she's still my sister. And she can tell the
rest of the family I'm okay."

He thought it over for a moment, then said, "All right, go
ahead and call her. You can use the car phone. But don't—"

"I know, I know. Don't tell her where I am." She picked
up the receiver and dialed Wendy's number. She heard
three rings, and then a woman's voice answered—a voice
she didn't recognize.

"Hayward residence."

"Hello, this is Nina. I'm Wendy's sister. Is she there?"

"I'm sorry, but Mr. and Mrs. Hayward are out for the evening. I'm the baby-sitter."

That's how worried she is about me, thought Nina with an irrational sense of abandonment.

"Would you like her to call you back?" asked the baby-sitter.

"No, I, uh, won't be available. But maybe I can call her later. Do you know what time she'll be home?"

"They're at the Brant Theater for that Legal Aid benefit. I think it runs till ten-thirty. And then they usually go out for coffee and dessert, so I'd expect them home around midnight."

"Oh. That's too late. I'll call tomorrow, thanks." She hung up and gave a sigh of disappointment.

"Not home?"

"No. I should have guessed they'd be out. In Jake's law firm, the business day doesn't end at five. The evenings are taken up by business affairs, too."

"Your brother-in-law's an attorney?"

"With ambitions of being a judge. And he's only thirty years old."

"Sounds like a fast-tracker."

"He is. Which means he needs a fast-track wife. Wendy's perfect that way. I'll bet you that right at this moment, she's at the theater charming the socks off some judge. And she can do it without even trying. She's the politician in the family." She glanced at Sam and saw that he was frowning. "Is something wrong?" she asked.

"What theater? Where did they go tonight?"

"The Brant Theater. That's where the benefit is."

"Benefit?"

"The baby-sitter said it was for Legal Aid. Why?"

Sam stared ahead at the road. "The Brant Theater. Didn't it just reopen?"

"A month ago. It was a disgrace before. All those porn flicks."

"Damn. Why didn't I think of it?"

Without warning, he made a screeching U-turn and headed the car the way they'd come, back toward the downtown district.

"What are you doing?" she demanded.

"The Brant Theater. A Legal Aid benefit. Who do you suppose'll be there?"

"A bunch of lawyers?"

"Right. As well as our esteemed D.A., Norm Liddell. Now, I'm not particularly fond of lawyers, but I'm not crazy about picking up their dead bodies, either."

She stared at him. "You think that's the target? The Brant Theater?"

"They'll need ushers tonight. Think about it. What does an usher wear?"

"Sometimes it's just black pants and a white shirt."

"But in a grand old theater like the Brant? They just might be dressed in green jackets with black braid...."

"That's where we're going?"

He nodded. "I want you to take a look. Tell me if we're warm. Tell me if that uniform you saw could've been a theater usher's."

By the time they pulled up across the street from the Brant Theater, it was 8:20. Sam didn't waste his time looking for a parking space; he left the car angled against the red-painted curb. As he and Nina climbed out, they heard a door-man yell, "Hey, you can't park there!"

"Police!" Sam answered, waving his badge. "We need to get in the theater."

The doorman stepped aside and waved them in.

The lobby was deserted. Through the closed aisle doors, they could hear the bluesy wail of clarinets, the syncopated beats of a snare drum. No ushers were in sight.

Sam yanked open an aisle door and slipped into the theater. Seconds later, he reemerged with a short and loudly protesting usher in tow. "Look at the uniform," he said to Nina. "Look familiar?"

Nina took one glance at the short green jacket, the black braid and brass buttons, and she nodded. "That's it. That's the one I saw."

"*What's* the one?" demanded the usher, yanking himself free.

"How many ushers working here tonight?" snapped Sam.

"Who are you, anyway?"

Again Sam whipped out his badge. "Police. There's a chance you have a bomb somewhere in there. So tell me quick. How many ushers?"

"A bomb?" The man's gaze darted nervously toward the lobby exit. "Uh, we got four working tonight."

"That's it?"

"Yeah. One didn't show up."

"Did he have a missing finger?"

"Hell, I don't know. We all wear gloves." The usher looked again toward the exit. "You really think there could be a bomb in there?"

"We can't afford to make a wrong guess. I'm evacuating the building." He glanced at Nina. "Get out of here. Wait in the car."

"But you'll need help—"

He was already pushing through the door, into the darkened theater. From the open doorway, she watched him walk swiftly down the aisle. He climbed up to the stage and crossed to the conductor, who regarded him with a look of startled outrage.

The musicians, just as startled, stopped playing.

Sam grabbed the conductor's microphone. "Ladies and gentlemen," he said curtly. "This is the Portland Police. We have had a bomb threat. Calmly, but without delay, will everyone please evacuate the building. I repeat, stay calm, but please evacuate the building."

Almost immediately the exodus began. Nina had to scramble backward out of the doorway to avoid the first rush of people heading up the aisle. In the confusion, she lost sight of Sam, but she could still hear his voice over the speaker system.

"Please remain calm. There is no immediate danger. Exit the building in an orderly fashion."

He's going to be the last one out, she thought. *The one most likely hurt if a bomb does go off.*

The exodus was in full force now, a rush of frightened men and women in evening clothes. The first hint of disaster happened so quickly Nina didn't even see it. Perhaps someone had tripped over a long hem; perhaps there were simply too many feet storming the doorway. Suddenly people were stumbling, falling over each other. A woman screamed. Those still backed up in the aisle instantly panicked.

And rushed for the door.

Eleven

Nina watched in horror as a woman in a long evening gown fell beneath the stampede. Struggling to reach her, Nina shoved through the crowd, only to be swept along with them and forced out the lobby doors and into the street. To get back inside the building was impossible; she'd be moving against the crowd, against the full force of panic.

Already the street was filling up with evacuees, everyone milling about looking dazed. To her relief, she caught sight of Wendy and Jake among the crowd; at least her sister was safe and out of the building. The flood of people out the doors gradually began to ebb.

But where was Sam? Had he made it out yet?

Then, through the crowd, she spotted him emerging from the lobby door. He had his arm around an elderly man, whom he hauled to the sidewalk and set down against the lamppost.

As Nina started toward him, Sam spotted her and yelled, "This one needs attention. Take care of him!"

"Where are you going?"

"Back inside. There are a few more in there."

"I can help you—"

"Help me by staying *out* of the building. And see to that man."

He has his job to do, she thought, watching Sam head back into the theater. *So do I.*

She turned her attention to the elderly man propped up against the lamppost. Kneeling beside him she asked, "Sir, are you all right?"

"My chest. It hurts…"

Oh, no. A coronary. And no ambulance in sight. At once she lowered his head onto the sidewalk, checked his pulse, and unbuttoned his shirt. She was so busy attending to her patient she scarcely noticed when the first patrol car pulled up in front of the theater. By then the crowd was a mass of confusion, everyone demanding to know what was going on.

She looked up to see Sam push out the lobby door again, this time carrying the woman in the evening dress. He lay the woman down beside Nina.

"One more inside," he said, turning back to the building. "Check the lady out."

"Navarro!" yelled a voice.

Sam glanced back as a man in a tuxedo approached.

"What the hell is going on?"

"Can't talk, Liddell. I've got work to do."

"Was there a bomb call or not?"

"Not a call."

"Then why'd you order an evacuation?"

"The usher's uniform." Again Sam turned toward the building.

"Navarro!" Liddell yelled. "I want an explanation! People have been hurt because of this! Unless you can justify it—"

Sam had vanished through the lobby doors.

Liddell paced the sidewalk, waiting to resume his harangue. At last, in frustration, he shouted, "I'm going to have your ass for this, Navarro!"

Those were the last words out of Liddell's mouth before the bomb exploded.

The force of the blast threw Nina backward, onto the street. She landed hard, her elbows scraping across the pavement, but she felt no pain. The shock of the impact left her too stunned to feel anything at all except a strange sense of unreality. She saw broken glass pelt the cars in the street. Saw smoke curl through the air and scores of people lying on the road, all of them just as stunned as she was. And she saw that the lobby door of the Brant Theater was tilted at a crazy angle and hanging by one hinge.

Through the pall of silence, she heard the first moan. Then another. Then came sobs, cries from the injured. Slowly she struggled to sit up. Only then did she feel the pain. Her elbows were torn and bleeding. Her head ached so badly she had to clutch it just to keep from throwing up. But as the awareness of pain crept into her consciousness, so too did the memory of what had happened just before the blast.

Sam. Sam had gone into the building.

Where was he? She scanned the road, the sidewalk, but her vision was blurry. She saw Liddell, sitting up now and groaning by the lamppost. Next to him was the elderly man whom Sam had dragged out of the theater. He, too, was conscious and moving. But there was no Sam.

She stumbled to her feet. A wave of dizziness almost sent her back down to her knees. Fighting it, she forced herself to move toward that open door and stepped inside.

It was dark, too dark to see anything. The only light was

the faint glow from the street, shining through the doorway. She stumbled across debris and landed on her knees. Quickly she rose back to her feet, but she knew it was hopeless. It was impossible to navigate, much less find anyone in this darkness.

"Sam?" she cried, moving deeper into the shadows. *"Sam?"*

Her own voice, thick with despair, echoed back at her.

She remembered that he'd stepped into the lobby a moment before the blast. He could be anywhere in the building, or he could be somewhere nearby. Somewhere she could reach him.

Again she cried out, "Sam!"

This time, faintly, she heard a reply. "Nina?" It didn't come from inside the building. It came from the outside. From the street.

She turned and felt her way back toward the exit, guided by the glow of the doorway. Even before she reached it, she saw him standing there, silhouetted in the light from the street.

"Nina?"

"I'm here. I'm here...." She stumbled through the last stretch of darkness dividing them and was instantly swept into an embrace that was too fierce to be gentle, too terrified to be comforting.

"What the hell were you doing in *there?*" he demanded.

"Looking for you."

"You were supposed to stay outside. Away from the building. When I couldn't find you..." His arms tightened around her, drawing her so close she felt as though it were his heart hammering in her chest. "Next time, you *listen* to me."

"I thought you were inside—"

"I came out the other door."

"I didn't see you!"

"I was dragging the last man out. I'd just got out when the bomb went off. It blew us both out onto the sidewalk." He pulled back and looked at her. Only then did she see the blood trickling down his temple.

"Sam, you need to see a doctor—"

"We have a lot of people here who need a doctor." He glanced around at the street. "I can wait."

Nina, too, focused on the chaos surrounding them. "We've got to get people triaged for the ambulances. I'll get to work."

"You feeling up to it?"

She gave him a nod. And a quick smile. "This is my forte, Detective. Disasters." She waded off into the crowd.

Now that she knew Sam was alive and safe, she could concentrate on what needed to be done. And one glance at the scene told her this was the start of a busy night. Not just here, in the street, but in the ER as well. All the area hospitals would need to call in every ER nurse they had to attend to these people.

Her head was starting to ache worse than ever, her scraped elbows stung every time she bent her arms. But at this moment, as far as she knew, she was the only nurse on the scene.

She focused on the nearest victim, a woman whose leg was cut and bleeding. Nina knelt down, ripped a strip of fabric from the victim's hem, and quickly wrapped a make-shift pressure bandage around the bleeding limb. When she'd finished tying it off, she noted to her satisfaction that the flow of blood had stopped.

That was only the first, she thought, and she looked around for the next patient. There were dozens more to go....

ACROSS THE STREET, his face hidden in the shadows, Vincent Spectre watched the chaos and muttered a curse. Both Judge Stanley Dalton and Norm Liddell were still alive. Spectre could see the young D.A. sitting against the lamppost, clutching his head. The blond woman sitting beside him must be Liddell's wife. They were right in the thick of things, surrounded by dozens of other injured theater patrons. Spectre couldn't just walk right over and dispatch Liddell, not without being seen by a score of witnesses. Sam Navarro was just a few yards from Liddell, and Navarro would certainly be armed.

Another humiliation. This would destroy his reputation, not to mention his back account. The Showman had promised four hundred thousand dollars for the deaths of Dalton and Liddell. Spectre had thought this an elegant solution: to kill both of them at once. With so many other victims, the identity of the targets might never be pinpointed.

But the targets were still alive, and there'd be no payment forthcoming.

The job had become too risky to complete, especially with Navarro on the scent. Thanks to Navarro, Spectre would have to bow out. And kiss his four hundred thousand goodbye.

He shifted his gaze, refocusing on another figure in the crowd. It was that nurse, Nina Cormier, bandaging one of the injured. This fiasco was her fault, too; he was sure of it. She must've given the police just enough info to tip them off to the bomb. The usher's uniform, no doubt, had been the vital clue.

She was another detail he hadn't bothered to clean up, and look at the result. No hit, no money. Plus, she could identify him. Though that police sketch was hopelessly generic, Spectre had a feeling that, if Nina Cormier ever saw his face, she would remember him. That made her a threat he could no longer ignore.

But now was not the opportunity. Not in this crowd, in this street. The ambulances were arriving, siren after siren whooping to a stop. And the police had cordoned off the street from stray vehicles.

Time to leave.

Spectre turned and walked away, his frustration mounting with every step he took. He'd always prided himself on paying attention to the little things. Anyone who worked with explosives had to have a fetish for details, or they didn't last long. Spectre intended to hang around in this business, which meant he would continue to fuss over the details.

And the next detail to attend to was Nina Cormier.

SHE WAS MAGNIFICENT. Sam paused wearily amid the broken glass and shouting voices and he gazed in Nina's direction. It was ten-thirty, an hour and a half since the explosion, and the street was still a scene of confusion. Police cars and ambulances were parked haphazardly up and down the block, their lights flashing like a dozen strobes. Emergency personnel were everywhere, picking through the wreckage, sorting through the victims. The most seriously injured had already been evacuated, but there were dozens more still to be transported to hospitals.

In the midst of all that wreckage, Nina seemed an island of calm efficiency. As Sam watched, she knelt down beside a groaning man and dressed his bleeding arm with a make-shift bandage. Then, with a reassuring pat and a soft word, she moved on to the next patient. As though sensing she was being watched, she suddenly glanced in Sam's direction. Just for a moment their gazes locked across the chaos, and she read the question in his eyes: *Are you holding up okay?*

She gave him a wave, a nod of reassurance. Then she turned back to her patient.

They both had their work cut out for them tonight. He focused his attention, once again, on the bomb scene investigation.

Gillis had arrived forty-five minutes ago with the personal body armor and mask. The rest of the team had straggled in one by one—three techs, Ernie Takeda, Detective Cooley. Even Abe Coopersmith had appeared, his presence more symbolic than practical. This was Sam's show, and everyone knew it. The bomb disposal truck was in place and parked nearby. Everyone was waiting.

It was time to go in the building. Time to search for any second device.

Sam and Gillis, both of them wearing headlamps, entered the theater.

The darkness made the search slow and difficult. Stepping gingerly over debris, Sam headed down the left aisle, Gillis the right. The back rows of seats had sustained damage only to the upholstery—shredded fabric and stuffing. The further they advanced the more severe the damage.

"Dynamite," Gillis noted, sniffing the air.

"Looks like the blast center's near the front."

Sam moved slowly toward the orchestra pit, the beam

of his headlamp slicing the darkness left and right as he scanned the area around the stage—or what had once been the stage. A few splintered boards was all that remained.

"Crater's right here," observed Gillis.

Sam joined him. The two men knelt down for a closer inspection. Like the church bomb a week before, this one was shallow—a low-velocity blast. Dynamite.

"Looks like the third row, center stage," said Sam. "Wonder who was sitting here."

"Assigned seating, you figure?"

"If so, then we'll have ourselves a convenient list of potential targets."

"Looks all clear to me," Gillis declared.

"We can call in the searchers." Sam rose to his feet and at once felt a little dizzy. The aftereffects of the blast. He'd been in so many bombs lately, his brain must be getting scrambled. Maybe some fresh air would clear his head.

"You okay?" asked Gillis.

"Yeah. I just need to get out of here for a moment." He stumbled back up the aisle and through the lobby doors. Outside he leaned against a lamppost, breathing gulps of night air. His dizziness faded and he became aware, once again, of the activity in the street. He noticed that the crowds had thinned, and that the injured had all been evacuated. Only one ambulance was still parked in the road.

Where was Nina?

That one thought instantly cleared his head. He glanced up and down the street, but caught no glimpse of her. Had she left the scene? Or was she taken from it?

A young cop manning the police line glanced up as Sam approached. "Yes, sir?"

"There was a woman—a nurse in street clothes—working out here. Where'd she go?"

"You mean the dark-haired lady? The pretty one?"

"That's her."

"She left in one of the ambulances, about twenty minutes ago. I think she was helping with a patient."

"Thanks." Sam went to his car and reached inside for his cellular phone. He was not taking any chances; he had to be sure she was safe. He dialed Maine Med ER.

The line was busy.

In frustration he climbed in the car. "I'm heading to the hospital!" he yelled to Gillis. "Be right back."

Ignoring his partner's look of puzzlement, Sam lurched away from the curb and steered through the obstacle course of police vehicles. Fifteen minutes later, he pulled into a parking stall near the hospital's emergency entrance.

Even before he walked in the doors, he could hear the sounds of frantic activity inside. The waiting area was mobbed. He pushed his way through the crowd until he'd reached the triage desk, manned by a clearly embattled nurse.

"I'm Detective Navarro, Portland Police," he said. "Is Nina Cormier working here?"

"Nina? Not tonight, as far as I know."

"She came in with one of the ambulances."

"I might have missed her. Let me check." She punched the intercom button and said, "There's a policeman out here. Wants to speak to Nina. If she's back there, can you ask her to come out?"

For a good ten minutes, he waited with growing impatience. Nina didn't appear. The crowd in the ER seemed to grow even larger, packing into every available square inch of the waiting area. Even worse, the reporters had shown up, TV cameras and all. The triage nurse had her hands full; she'd forgotten entirely about Sam.

Unable to wait any longer, he pushed past the front desk. The nurse was calming down a hysterical family member; she didn't even notice Sam had crossed into the inner sanctum and was heading up the ER corridor.

Treatment rooms lined both sides of the halls. He glanced in each one as he passed. All were occupied and overflowing with victims from the bombing. He saw stunned faces, bloodied clothes. But no Nina.

He turned, retraced his steps down the hall, and paused outside a closed door. It was the trauma room. From beyond the door came the sound of voices, the clang of cabinets. He knew that a crisis was in full swing, and he was reluctant to intrude, but he had no alternative. He had to confirm that Nina was here, that she'd made it safely to the ER.

He pushed open the door.

A patient—a man—was lying on the table, his body white and flaccid under the lights. Half a dozen medical personnel were laboring over him, one performing CPR, the others scurrying about with IV's and drugs. Sam paused, momentarily stunned by the horror of the scene.

"*Sam?*"

Only then did he notice Nina moving toward him from the other side of the room. Like all the other nurses, she was dressed in scrub clothes. He hadn't even noticed her in that first glimpse of blue-clad personnel.

She took his arm and quickly tugged him out of the room. "What are you doing here?" she whispered.

"You left the blast site. I wasn't sure what happened to you."

"I rode here in one of the ambulances. I figured they needed me." She glanced back at the door to the trauma room. "I was right."

"Nina, you can't just take off without telling me! I had no idea if you were all right."

She regarded him with an expression of quiet wonder, but didn't say a thing.

"Are you listening to me?" he said.

"Yes," she replied softly. "But I don't believe what I'm hearing. You actually sound scared."

"I wasn't scared. I was just— I mean—" He shook his head in frustration. "Okay, I was worried. I didn't want something to happen to you."

"Because I'm your witness?"

He looked into her eyes, those beautiful, thoughtful eyes. Never in his life had he felt so vulnerable. This was a new feeling for him and he didn't like it. He was not a man who was easily frightened, and the fact that he had experienced such fear at the thought of losing her told him he was far more deeply involved than he'd ever intended to be.

"Sam?" She reached up and touched his face.

He grasped her hand and gently lowered it. "Next time," he instructed, "I want you to tell me where you're going. It's *your* life at stake. If you want to risk it, that's your business. But until Spectre's under arrest, your safety's my concern. Do you understand?"

She withdrew her hand from his. The retreat was more than physical; he could feel her pulling away emotionally as well, and it hurt him. It was a pain of his own choosing, and that made it even worse.

She said, tightly, "I understand perfectly well."

"Good. Now, I think you should go back to the hotel where we can keep an eye on you tonight."

"I can't leave. They need me here."

"I need you, too. Alive."

"Look at this place!" She waved toward the waiting area, crowded with the injured. "These people all have to be examined and treated. I can't walk out now."

"Nina, I have a job to do. And your safety is part of that job."

"I have a job to do, too!" she asserted.

They faced each other for a moment, neither one willing to back down.

Then Nina snapped, "I don't have time for this," and she turned back toward the trauma room.

"Nina!"

"I'll do my job, Sam. You do yours."

"Then I'm sending a man over to keep an eye on you."

"Do whatever you want."

"When will you be finished here?"

She stopped and glanced at the waiting patients. "My guess? Not till morning."

"Then I'll be back to get you at 6:00 a.m."

"Whatever you say, Detective," she retorted and pushed into the trauma room. He caught a fleeting glimpse of her as she rejoined the surgical team, and then the door closed behind her.

I'll do my job. You do yours, she'd told him.

She's right, he thought. *That's exactly what I should be focusing on. My job.*

From his car phone, he put in a call to Officer Pressler and told him to send his relief officer down to Maine Med ER, where he'd be the official baby-sitting service for the night. Then, satisfied that Nina was in good hands, he headed back to the bomb scene.

It was eleven-thirty. The night was just beginning.

NINA MADE IT THROUGH the next seven hours on sheer nerve. Her conversation with Sam had left her hurt and angry, and she had to force herself to concentrate on the work at hand—tending to the dozens of patients who now filled the waiting area. Their injuries, their discomfort, had to take priority. But every so often, when she'd pause to collect her thoughts or catch her breath, she'd find herself thinking about Sam, about what he'd said.

I have a job to do. And your safety is part of that job.

Is that all I am to you? she wondered as she signed her name to yet another patient instruction sheet. A job, a burden? And what had she expected, anyway? From the beginning, he'd been the unflappable public official, Mr. Cool himself. There'd been flashes of warmth, of course, even the occasional glimpse of the man inside, a man of genuine kindness. But every time she thought she'd touched the real Sam Navarro, he'd pull away from her as though scalded by the contact.

What am I to do with you, Sam? she wondered sadly. And what was she to do with all the feelings she had for him?

Work was all that kept her going that night. She never even noticed when the sun came up.

By the time 6:00 a.m. rolled around, she was so tired she could scarcely walk without weaving, but at last the waiting room was empty and the patients all sent home. Most of the ER staff had gathered, shell-shocked, in the employee lounge for a well-deserved coffee break. Nina was about to join them when she heard her name called.

She turned. Sam was standing in the waiting room.

He looked every bit as exhausted as she felt, his eyes bleary, his jaw dark with a day's growth of beard. At her first sight of his face, all the anger she'd felt the night before instantly evaporated.

My poor, poor Sam, she thought. *You give so much of yourself. And what comfort do you have at the end of the day?*

She went to him. He didn't speak; he just looked at her with that expression of weariness. She put her arms around him. For a moment they held each other, their bodies trembling with fatigue. Then she heard him say, softly, "Let's go home."

"I'd like that," she said. And smiled.

She didn't know how he managed to pilot the car to his house. All she knew was that a moment after she dozed off, they were in his driveway, and he was gently prodding her awake. Together they dragged themselves into the house, into his bedroom. No thoughts of lust crossed her mind, even as they undressed and crawled into bed together, even as she felt his lips brush her face, felt his breath warm her hair.

She fell asleep in his arms.

SHE FELT SO WARM, so perfect, lying beside him. As if she belonged here, in his bed.

Sam gazed through drowsy eyes at Nina, who was still sound asleep. It was already afternoon. He should have been up and dressed hours ago, but sheer exhaustion had taken its toll.

He was getting too old for this job. For the past eighteen years, he'd been a cop through and through. Though there were times when he hated the work, when the ugly side of it seemed to overwhelm his love for the job, he'd never once doubted that a cop was exactly what he was meant to be. And so it dismayed him now that, at this moment, being a cop was the furthest thing from his mind.

What he wanted, really wanted, was to spend eternity in this bed, gazing at this woman. Studying her face, enjoying the view. Only when Nina was asleep did he feel it was safe to really look at her. When she was awake, he felt too vulnerable, as though she could read his thoughts, could see past his barriers, straight to his heart. He was afraid to admit, even to himself, the feelings he harbored there.

As he studied her now, he realized there was no point denying it to himself: he couldn't bear the thought of her walking out of his life. Did that mean he loved her? He didn't know.

He did know this was not the turn of events he'd wanted or expected.

But last night he'd watched her at work in the wreckage of the bomb site, and he'd admired a new dimension of Nina, one he saw for the first time. A woman with both compassion and strength.

It would be so easy to fall in love with her. It would be such a mistake.

In a month, a year, she'd come to see him for what he was: no hero with a badge, but an everyday guy doing his job the best way he knew how. And there she'd be in that hospital, working side by side with men like Robert Bledsoe. Men with medical degrees and houses on the water. How long would it take for her to grow weary of the cop who just happened to love her?

He sat up on the side of the bed and ran his hands through his hair, trying to shake off the last vestiges of sleep. His brain wasn't feeling alert yet. He needed coffee, food, anything to snap him back into gear. There were so many details to follow up on, so many leads still to check out.

Then he felt a touch, soft as silk, caress his bare back. All at once, work was the last thing on his mind.

He turned and met her gaze. She was looking drowsily at him, her smile relaxed and contented. "What time is it?" she murmured.

"Almost three."

"We slept that long?"

"We needed it. Both of us. It was okay to let our guard down. Pressler was watching the house."

"You mean he was outside all day?"

"I made the arrangements last night. Before he went off duty. I knew I wanted to bring you home with me."

She opened her arms to him. That gesture of invitation was too tempting to resist. With a groan of surrender, he lay down beside her and met her lips with a kiss. At once his body was responding, and so was she. Their arms were entwined now, their warmth mingling. He couldn't stop, couldn't turn back; he wanted her too badly. He wanted to feel their bodies join, just one last time. If he couldn't have her for the rest of his life, at least he would have her for this moment. And he'd remember, always, her face, her smile, her sweet moans of desire as he thrust, hard and deep, inside her.

They both took. They both gave.

But even as he reached his climax, even as he felt the first glorious release, he thought, *This is not enough. This could never be enough.* He wanted to know more than just her body; he wanted to know her soul.

His passion was temporarily sated, yet he felt both un-satisfied and depressed as he lay beside her afterward. Not at all what the carefree bachelor should expect to feel after a conquest. If anything, he was angry at himself for sliding into this situation. For allowing this woman to become so important to him.

And here she was, smiling, working her way even deeper into his life.

His response was to pull away, to rise from the bed and head into the shower. When he reemerged, clean and still damp, she was sitting up on the side of the bed, watching him with a look of bewilderment.

"I have to get back to work," he said, pulling on a clean shirt. "I'll invite Pressler inside to sit with you."

"The bombing's over and done with. Spectre's probably a thousand miles away by now."

"I can't take that chance."

"There are others who know his face. The theater ushers. They could identify him."

"One of them hit his head on the sidewalk. He's still in and out of consciousness. The other one can't even decide on the color of Spectre's eyes. That's how helpful the ushers are."

"Nevertheless, you've got other witnesses and Spectre knows it." She paused. "I'd say that lets both of us off the hook."

"What do you mean?"

"I can stop worrying about being a target. And you can stop worrying about keeping me alive. And go back to your real job."

"This is part of my job."

"So you've told me." She tilted her chin up, and he saw

the brief gleam of tears in her eyes. "I wish I was more than that. God, I wish…"

"Nina, please. This doesn't help either one of us."

Her head drooped. The sight of her, hurt, silent, was almost more than he could stand. He knelt down before her and took her hands in his. "You know I'm attracted to you."

She gave a softly ironic laugh. "That much, I guess, is obvious to us both."

"And you also know that I think you're a terrific woman. If I ever get hauled to the ER in an ambulance, I hope you're the nurse who takes care of me."

"But?"

"But…" He sighed. "I just don't see us together. Not for the long haul."

She looked down again, and he could sense her struggle for composure. He'd hurt her, and he hated himself for it, hated his own cowardice. That's what it was, of course. He didn't believe hard enough in their chances. He didn't believe in *her.*

All he was certain of was that he'd never, ever get over her.

He rose to his feet. She didn't react, but just sat on the bed, staring down. "It's not you, Nina," he said. "It's *me.* It's something that happened to me years ago. It convinced me that this situation we're in—it doesn't last. It's artificial. A scared woman. And a cop. It's a setup for all kinds of unrealistic expectations."

"Don't give me the old psychology lecture, Sam. I don't need to hear about transference and misplaced affections."

"You have to hear it. And understand it. Because the effect goes both ways. How you feel about me, and how I feel about you. My wanting to take care of you, protect you. It's something I can't help, either." He sighed, a sound of both frustration and despair. *It's too late,* he thought. *We both feel things we shouldn't be feeling. And it's impossible to turn back the clock.*

"You were saying something happened to you. Years ago," she said. "Was it…another woman?"

He nodded.

"The same situation? Scared woman, protective cop?" Again he nodded.

"Oh." She shook her head and murmured in a tone of self-disgust, "I guess I fell right into it."

"We both did."

"So who left whom, Sam? The last time this happened?"

"It was the only time it happened. Except for you." He turned away, began to move around the room. "I was just a rookie patrolman. Twenty-two years old. Assigned to protect a woman being stalked. She was twenty-eight going on forty when it came to sophistication. It's not surprising I got a little infatuated. The surprising part was that she seemed to return the sentiment. At least, until the crisis was over. Then she decided I wasn't so impressive after all. And she was right." He stopped and looked at her. "It's that damn thing called reality. It has a way of stripping us all down to what we really are. And in my case, I'm just a hardworking cop. Honest for the most part. Brighter than some, dumber than others. In short, I'm not anyone's hero. And when she finally saw that, she turned right around and walked out, leaving behind one sadder but wiser rookie."

"And you think that's what I'm going to do."

"It's what you should do. Because you deserve so much, Nina. More than I can ever give you."

She shook her head. "What I really want, Sam, has nothing to do with what a man can *give* me."

"Think about Robert. What you could have had with him."

"Robert was the perfect example! He had it all. Everything except what I wanted from him."

"What did you want, Nina?"

"Love. Loyalty." She met his gaze. "Honesty."

What he saw in her eyes left him shaken. Those were the things he wanted to give her. The very things he was afraid to give her.

"Right now you think it's enough," he remarked. "But maybe you'll find out it's not."

"It's more than I ever got from Robert." *More than I'll ever get from you, too,* was what her eyes said.

He didn't try to convince her otherwise. Instead, he turned toward the door.

"I'm going to call Pressler inside," he told her. "Have him stay with you all day today."

"There's no need."

"You shouldn't be alone, Nina."

"I won't be." She looked up at him. "I can go back to my father's house. He has that fancy security system. Not to mention a few dogs. Now that we know Daniella isn't the one running around planting bombs, I should be perfectly safe there." She glanced around the room. "I shouldn't be staying here, anyway. Not in your house."

"You can. As long as you need to."

"No." She met his gaze. "I don't really see the point, Sam. Since it's so apparent to us both that this is a hopeless relationship."

He didn't argue with her. And that, more than anything else, was what hurt her. He could see it in her face.

He simply said, "I'll drive you there." Then he turned and left the room. He had to.

He couldn't bear to see the look in her eyes.

Twelve

"We think we know who the target was," reported Sam. "It was our wonderful D.A., Liddell."

Chief Coopersmith stared across the conference table at Sam and Gillis. "Are you certain?"

"Everything points that way. We pinpointed the bomb placement to somewhere in Row Three, Seats G through J. The seating last night was reserved weeks in advance. We've gone over the list of people sitting in that row and section. And Liddell and his wife were right smack in the center. They would've been killed instantly."

"Who else was in that row?"

"Judge Dalton was about six seats away," said Gillis. "Chances are, he would've been killed, too. Or at least seriously maimed."

"And the other people in that row?"

"We've checked them all out. A visiting law professor from California. A few relatives of Judge Dalton's. A pair of law clerks. We doubt any of them would've attracted the interest of a hired killer. Oh, and you may be interested to hear Ernie Takeda's latest report. He called it in from the lab this afternoon. It was dynamite, Dupont label. Prima detonating cord. Green electrical tape."

"Spectre," said Coopersmith. He leaned back and exhaled a loud sigh of weariness. They were all tired. Every one of them had worked straight through the night, caught a few hours of sleep, and then returned to the job. Now it was 5:00 p.m., and another night was just beginning. "God, the man is back with a vengeance."

"Yeah, but he's not having much luck," commented Gillis. "His targets keep surviving. Liddell. Judge Dalton. Nina Cormier. I'd say that the legendary Vincent Spectre must be feeling pretty frustrated about now."

"Embarrassed, too," added Sam. "His reputation's on the line, if it isn't already shot. After this fiasco, he's washed up as a contract man. Anyone with the money to hire will go elsewhere."

"Do we know who *did* hire him?"

Sam and Gillis glanced at each other. "We can make a wild guess," said Gillis.

"Billy Binford?"

Sam nodded. "The Snowman's trial is coming up in a month. And Liddell was dead set against any plea bargains. Rumor has it, he was going to use a conviction as a jumping-off place for some political campaign. I think The Snowman knows he's in for a long stay in jail. I think he wants Liddell off the prosecution team. Permanently."

"If Sam hadn't cleared that theater," added Gillis, "we could have lost half our prosecutors. The courts would've been backed up for months. In that situation, Binford's lawyers could've written the plea bargain for him."

"Any way we can pin this down with proof?"

"Not yet. Binford's attorney, Albert Darien, denies any knowledge of this. We're not going to be able to shake a word out of him. ATF's going over the videotapes from the prison surveillance cameras, looking over all the visitors that Binford had. We may be able to identify a go-between."

"You think it's someone other than his attorney?"

"Possibly. If we can identify that go-between, we may have a link to Spectre."

"Go for it," said Coopersmith. "I want this guy, and I want him bad."

At five-thirty, the meeting broke up and Sam headed for the coffee machine in search of a caffeine boost that would keep him going for the next eight hours. He was just taking his first sip when Norm Liddell walked into the station. Sam couldn't help feeling a prick of satisfaction at the sight of the bruises and scrapes on Liddell's face. The injuries were minor, but last night, after the bomb, Liddell had been among those screaming the loudest for medical assistance. His own wife, who'd sustained a broken arm, had finally told her husband to shut up and act like a man.

Now here he was, sporting a few nasty scrapes on his face as well as a look of—could it be? Contrition?

"Afternoon, Navarro," said Liddell, his voice subdued.

"Afternoon."

"I, uh…" Liddell cleared his throat and glanced around the hall, as though to check if anyone was listening. No one was.

"How's the wife doing?" asked Sam.

"Fine. She'll be in a cast for a while. Luckily, it was just a closed fracture."

"She handled herself pretty well last night, considering her injury," Sam commented. *Unlike you.*

"Yes, well, my wife's got a spine of steel. In fact, that's sort of why I want to talk to you."

"Oh?"

"Look, Navarro. Last night…I guess I jumped on you prematurely. I mean, I didn't realize you had information about any bomb."

Sam didn't say a word. He didn't want to interrupt this enjoyable performance.

"So when I got on your case last night—about evacuating the building—I should've realized you had your reasons. But damn it, Navarro, all I could see was all those people hurt in the stampede. I thought you'd gotten them panicked for nothing, and I—" He paused, obviously struggling to bite back his words. "Anyway, I apologize."

"Apology accepted."

Liddell gave a curt nod of relief.

"Now you can tell your wife you're off the hook."

The look on Liddell's face was all Sam needed to know that he'd guessed right. This apology had been Mrs. Liddell's idea, bless her steely spine. He couldn't help grinning as he watched the other man turn and walk stiffly toward Chief Coopersmith's office. The good D.A., it appeared, was not the one wearing the pants in the family.

"Hey, Sam!" Gillis was heading toward him, pulling on his jacket. "Let's go."

"Where?"

"Prison's got a surveillance videotape they want us to look at. It's The Snowman and some unknown visitor from a few days ago."

Sam felt a sudden adrenaline rush. "Was it Spectre?"

"No. It was a woman."

"THERE. THE BLONDE," said Detective Cooley.

Sam and Gillis leaned toward the TV screen, their gazes fixed on the black-and-white image of the woman. The view of her face was intermittently blocked by other visitors moving in the foreground, but from what they could see, the woman was indeed a blonde, twenties to thirties, and built like a showgirl.

"Okay, freeze it there," Cooley said to the video tech. "That's a good view of her."

The woman was caught in a still frame, her face turned to the surveillance camera, her figure momentarily visible between two passersby. She was dressed in a skirt suit, and she appeared to be carrying a briefcase. Judging by her attire, she might be an attorney or some other professional. But two details didn't fit.

One was her shoes. The camera's angle, facing downward, captured a view of her right foot, perched atop a sexy spike-heeled sandal with a delicate ankle strap.

"Not the kind of shoes you wear to court," noted Sam.

"Not unless you're out to give the judge a thrill," Gillis said. "And look at that makeup."

It was the second detail that didn't fit. This woman was made up like no lawyer Sam had ever seen. Obviously false eyelashes. Eyeshadow like some tropical fish. Lipstick painted on in bold, broad smears.

"Man, she sure ain't the girl next door," Gillis observed.

"What's the name on the visitor log?" asked Sam.

Cooley glanced at a sheet of paper. "She signed in as Marilyn Dukoff. Identified her purpose for visiting The Snowman as attorney-client consultation."

Gillis laughed. "If she's an attorney, then I'm applying to law school."

"Which law firm did she say she was with?" asked Sam.

"Frick and Darien."

"Not true?"

Cooley shook his head. "She's not on the firm's list of partners, associates or clerks. But…" He leaned forward, a grin on his face. "We think we know where she *did* work."

"Where?"

"The Stop Light."

Gillis shot Sam a look of *Didn't I tell ya?* No one had to explain a thing. They knew all about the Stop Light and its stage shows, pasties optional.

"Let me guess," said Sam. "Exotic dancer."

"You got it," affirmed Cooley.

"Are we sure we're talking about the right Marilyn Dukoff?"

"I think we are," Cooley answered. "See, all visitors to the prison have to present ID, and that's the name she gave, backed up by a Maine driver's license. We've pulled the license file. And here's the photo." Cooley passed a copy of the photo to Sam and Gillis.

"It's her," said Gillis.

"Which means we're talking about the right Marilyn Dukoff," said Cooley. "I think she just waltzed in under her own name and didn't bother with fake IDs. All she faked was her profession."

"Which is obviously not in the legal field," Gillis drawled.

Sam gave a nod to Cooley. "Good work."

"Unfortunately," added the younger detective, "I can't seem to locate the woman herself. We know where she *was* employed, but she left the job two weeks ago. I sent a man to the address listed on her license. She doesn't answer the door. And her phone's just been disconnected." He paused. "I think it's time for a search warrant."

"Let's get it." Sam rose to his feet and glanced at Gillis. "Meet you in the car, ten minutes."

"The blonde's?"

"Unless you've got somewhere better to go."

Gillis looked back at the video screen. At that still shot of a slim ankle, a sexy shoe. "Better than *that?*" He laughed. "I don't think so."

THE POLICE WERE getting too close for comfort.

Spectre slouched in the doorway of an apartment building half a block away and watched the cops come out of Marilyn's old building. Only moments before, Spectre had been inside that apartment, checking to make sure Marilyn hadn't left behind any clues to her current whereabouts. Luckily for him, he'd slipped out just ahead of Navarro's arrival.

They'd been inside almost an hour. They were good, all right—but Spectre was cleverer. Hours after the theater bombing, he'd hustled Marilyn into a different apartment across town. He'd known that his target might become apparent once they'd pinpointed the bomb placement in the theater. And that Marilyn would inevitably come under their scrutiny. Luckily, she'd been cooperative.

Unfortunately, her usefulness was just about over, and the time had come to end their association. But first, he needed her for one more task.

His face tightened as he spotted a familiar figure emerge from the building. Navarro again. The detective had come to represent all the failures that Spectre had suffered over the past week. Navarro was the brains behind the investigation, the one man responsible for Liddell still being alive.

No hit. No fee. Navarro had cost him money—a lot of it.

Spectre watched the cops confer on the sidewalk. There were five of them, three in plain clothes, two in uniform, but it was Navarro on whom he focused his rage. This had turned into a battle of wits between them, a test of determination. In all his years as a "fuse" man, Spectre had never matched skills with such a wily opponent.

The safe thing to do was merely to slip away from this town and seek out contracts elsewhere. Miami or New Orleans. But his reputation had suffered a serious blow here; he wasn't sure he could land a job in Miami. And he had the feeling Navarro wouldn't give up the pursuit, that, wherever Spectre went, the detective would be dogging his trail.

And then, there was the matter of getting even. Spectre wasn't going to walk away without exacting some kind of payback.

The three plainclothes cops climbed into an unmarked car and drove away. A moment later, the uniformed cops were gone as well. They had found nothing in Marilyn's apartment; Spectre had seen to it.

Catch me if you can, Navarro, he thought. *Or will I catch you first?*

He straightened and stamped his feet, feeling the blood return to his legs. Then he left the doorway and walked around the corner, to his car.

Navarro. Once and for all, he had to take care of Navarro. And he had the perfect plan. It would require Marilyn's help. One little phone call—that's all he'd ask. And then he'd ask no more of her.

Ever again.

THE DINNER WAS EXCELLENT. The company was wretched.

Daniella, dressed in an iridescent green leotard and a slinky wraparound skirt, sullenly picked at her salad, ignoring the platter of roast duckling and wild rice. She was not speaking to her husband, and he was not speaking to her, and Nina was too uncomfortable to speak to either one of them.

After all those questions by the police, the matter of Daniella's affair with Robert had come to light. While Nina would never forgive Daniella for that betrayal, at least she could manage to pull off a civil evening with the woman.

Nina's father could not. He was still in a state of shock from the revelation. His showpiece wife, the stunning blonde thirty years his junior, had not been satisfied with marrying mere wealth. She'd wanted a younger man. After four marriages, George Cormier still didn't know how to choose the right wife.

Now it looks like this will be his fourth divorce, Nina thought. She glanced at her father, then at Daniella. Though she loved her father, she couldn't help feeling that he and Daniella deserved each other. In the worst possible way.

Daniella set down her fork. "If you'll excuse me," she said, "I don't really have much of an appetite. I think I'll skip out for a movie."

"What about me?" snapped George. "I know I'm just your husband, but a few evenings a week with your boring old spouse isn't too much to ask, is it? Considering all the benefits you get in exchange."

"Benefits? *Benefits?*" Daniella drew herself to her feet

in anger. "All the money in the world can't make up for being married to an old goat like you."

"*Goat?*"

"An old goat. Do you hear me? *Old.*" She leaned across the table. "In every sense of the word."

He, too, rose to his feet. "Why, you bitch…"

"Go ahead. Call me names. I can think of just as many to call you back." With a whisk of her blond hair, she turned and walked out of the dining room.

George stared after her for a moment. Slowly, he sank back in his chair. "God," he whispered. "What was I thinking when I married her?"

You weren't thinking at all, Nina felt like saying. She touched her father's arm. "Seems like neither one of us is any good at picking spouses. Are we, Dad?"

He regarded his daughter with a look of shared misery. "I sincerely hope you haven't inherited my bad luck with love, sweetheart."

They sat for a moment without speaking. Their supper lay, almost untouched, on the table. In another room, music had started up, the fast and thumping rhythm of an aerobics tape. Daniella was at it again, working off her anger by sculpting a new and better body. Smart girl; she was going to come out of a divorce looking like a million bucks.

Nina sighed and leaned back. "Whether it's bad luck or character flaws, Dad, maybe some people are just meant to be single."

"Not you, Nina. You *need* to love someone. You always have. And that's what makes you so easy to love."

She gave a sad laugh but said nothing. *Easy to love, easy to leave,* she thought.

Once again, she found herself wondering what Sam

was doing. What he was thinking. Not about her, surely; he was too much the cop to be bothered by minor distractions.

Yet when the phone rang, she couldn't suppress the sudden hope that he was calling. She sat at the table, heart thumping hard as she listened to Daniella's voice in the next room talking on the phone.

A moment later, Daniella appeared in the doorway and said, "It's for you, Nina. The hospital. They said they've been trying to reach you."

Disappointed, Nina rose to take the call. "Hello?"

"Hi, this is Gladys Power, the night nursing supervisor. Sorry to bother you—we got your phone number from your mother. We have a number of staff out sick tonight, and we were wondering if you could come in to cover for the ER."

"Night shift?"

"Yes. We could really use you."

Nina glanced toward Daniella's exercise room, where the music was playing louder than ever. She had to get out of this house. Away from this emotional battleground.

She said, "Okay, I'll take the shift."

"See you at eleven o'clock."

"Eleven?" Nina frowned. The night shift usually started at midnight. "You want me there an hour early?"

"If you could manage it. We're shorthanded on the evening shift as well."

"Right. I'll be there, eleven o'clock." She hung up and breathed a soft sigh of relief. Work was exactly what she needed. Maybe eight hours of crises, major and minor, would get her mind back on track.

And off the subject of Sam Navarro.

MARILYN HUNG UP THE PHONE. "She said she'd be there."

Spectre gave a nod of approval. "You handled it well."

"Of course." Marilyn favored him with that satisfied smile of hers. A smile that said, *I'm worth every penny you pay me.*

"Did she seem at all suspicious?" he asked.

"Not a bit. I'm telling you, she'll be there. Eleven o'clock, just like you wanted." Marilyn tilted back her head and gave her lips a predatory lick. "Now, do I get what I want?"

He smiled. "What *do* you want?"

"You know." She sidled toward him and unbuckled his belt. His breath caught in an involuntary gasp as that hot little hand slid inside his trousers. Her touch was delicious, expert, her technique designed to reduce a man to begging. Oh yes, he knew exactly what she was asking for.

And it wasn't sex.

Why not enjoy the moment? he thought. She was willing, and he still had the time to spare. Three hours until Nina Cormier showed up for her shift at the hospital. Some quick amusement with Marilyn, and then on to more serious business.

She dropped to her knees before him. "You said you'd pay me what I was worth," she whispered.

He groaned. "I promised…"

"I'm worth a lot. Don't you think?"

"Absolutely."

"I can be worth even more to you."

He gave a jerk of pleasure and grasped her face. Breathing heavily, he stroked down her cheek, her jaw, to her neck. Such a long, slender neck. How easy it should be to finish it. First, though, he'd let *her* finish…

"Oh, yes," she murmured. "You're ready for me."

He pulled her, hard, against him. And he thought, *A pity you won't be ready for me.*

IT WAS TEN-THIRTY by the time a weary Sam stepped through his front door. The first thing he noticed was the silence. The emptiness. It was a house that had somehow lost its soul.

He turned on the lights, but even the glow of all those lamps couldn't seem to dispel the shadows. For the past three years, this was the house he'd called home, the house he'd returned to every evening after work. Now the place felt cold to him, like the house of a stranger. Not a home at all.

He poured himself a glass of milk and drank it in a few thirsty gulps. So much for supper; he didn't have the energy to cook. He poured a second glass and carried it over to the telephone. All evening, he'd been itching to make this call, but something had always interrupted him. Now that he had a few blessed moments of peace, he was going to call Nina. He was going to tell her what he'd been afraid to tell her, what he could no longer deny to her, or to himself.

It had come to him this afternoon, a realization that had struck him, oddly enough, in the midst of searching Marilyn Dukoff's apartment. He'd stood in the woman's bedroom and gazed at the empty bureau drawers, the stripped mattress. And without warning, he'd been struck by a sense of loneliness so intense it made his chest ache. Because that abandoned room had suddenly come to represent his life. It had a purpose, a function, but it was nevertheless empty.

I've been a cop too long, he'd thought. *I've let it take over my life.* Only at that moment, standing in that empty bedroom, did it occur to him how little of his own life he really had. No wife, no kids, no family.

Nina had opened his eyes to the possibilities. Yes, he was scared. Yes, he knew just how much, how deeply, he would be hurt if she ever left him. But the alternative was just as bleak; that he would never even give it a chance.

He'd been a coward. But no longer.

He picked up the phone and dialed Nina's father's house.

A few rings later, the call was answered by a bland "Hello?" Not Nina but Daniella, the fitness freak.

"This is Sam Navarro," he said. "Sorry to call so late. May I speak to Nina?"

"She's not here."

His immediate pang of disappointment was quickly followed by a cop's sense of dismay. How could she not be there? She was supposed to stay in a safe place tonight, not run around unprotected.

"Mind telling me where she went?" he asked.

"The hospital. They called her in to work the night shift."

"The Emergency Room?"

"I guess so."

"Thanks." He hung up, his disappointment so heavy it felt like a physical weight on his shoulders. What the hell. He was not going to hold off any longer. He was going to tell her now. Tonight.

He dialed Maine Medical ER.

"Emergency Room."

"This is Detective Sam Navarro, Portland Police. May I speak with Nina Cormier?"

"Nina's not here tonight."

"Well, when she gets there, could you ask her to call me at home?"

"She's not scheduled to come in."

"Excuse me?"

"I have the time sheet right in front of me. Her name's not down here for tonight."

"I was told someone called her in to work the night shift."

"I don't know anything about that."

"Well, can you find out? This is urgent."

"Let me check with the supervisor. Can you hold?"

In the silence that followed, Sam could hear his own blood rushing through his ears. Something was wrong. That old instinct of his was tingling.

The woman came back on the line. "Detective? I've checked with the supervisor. She says she doesn't know anything about it, either. According to her schedule, Nina isn't listed for any shifts until next week."

"Thank you," said Sam softly.

For a moment he sat thinking about that phone call from the hospital. Someone had known enough to locate Nina at her father's house. Someone had talked her into leaving those protective gates at an hour of night when there'd be few witnesses to see what was about to happen.

Not just someone. Spectre.

It was 10:45.

In a heartbeat, he was out the door and running to his car. Even as he roared out of his driveway, he knew he might already be too late. Racing for the freeway, he steered with one hand and dialed his car phone with the other.

"Gillis here," answered a weary voice.

"I'm on my way to Maine Med," Sam said. "Spectre's there."

"What?"

"Nina got a bogus call asking her to come in to work. I'm sure it was him. She's already left the house—"

Gillis replied, "I'll meet you there," and hung up.

Sam turned his full attention to the road. The speedometer hit seventy. Eighty.

Don't let me be too late, he prayed.

He floored the accelerator.

THE HOSPITAL PARKING garage was deserted, a fact that scarcely concerned Nina as she drove through the automatic gate. She had often been in this garage late at night, either coming to, or leaving from, her shifts in the ER, and she'd never encountered any problems. Portland, after all, was one of the safest towns in America.

Provided you're not on someone's hit list, she reminded herself.

She pulled into a parking stall and sat there for a moment, trying to calm her nerves. She wanted to start her shift with her mind focused clearly on the job. Not on death threats. Not on Sam Navarro. Once she walked in those doors, she was first and foremost a professional. People's lives depended on it.

She opened the door and stepped out of the car.

It was still an hour before the usual shift change. Come midnight, this garage would be busy with hospital staff coming or going. But at this moment, no one else was around. She quickened her pace. The hospital elevator was just ahead; the way was clear. Only a dozen yards to go.

She never saw the man step out from behind the parked car.

But she felt a hand grasp her arm, felt the bite of a gun barrel pressed against her temple. Her scream was cut off by the first words he uttered.

"Not a sound or you're dead." The gun at her head was all the emphasis needed to keep her silent.

He yanked her away from the elevator, shoved her toward a row of parked cars. She caught a fleeting glimpse of his face as she was spun around. *Spectre.* They were moving now, Nina sobbing as she stumbled forward, the man gripping her arm with terrifying strength.

He's going to kill me now, here, where no one will see it....

The pounding of her own pulse was so loud at first, she didn't hear the faint squeal of tires across pavement.

But her captor did. Spectre froze, his grip still around her arm.

Now Nina heard it, too: car tires, screeching up the garage ramp.

With savage force, Spectre wrenched her sideways, toward the cover of a parked car. *This is my only chance to escape,* she thought.

In an instant she was fighting back, struggling against his grip. He was going to shoot her anyway. Whether it happened in some dark corner or out here, in the open, she would not go down without a fight. She kicked, flailed, clawed at his face.

He swung at her, a swift, ugly blow that slammed against her chin. The pain was blinding. She staggered, felt herself falling. He grasped her arm and began dragging her across the pavement. She was too stunned to fight now, to save herself.

Light suddenly glared in her eyes, a light so bright it seemed to stab straight through her aching head. She heard tires screech and realized she was staring at a pair of headlights.

A voice yelled, *"Freeze!"*

Sam. It was Sam.

"Let her go, Spectre!" Sam shouted.

The gun barrel was back at Nina's head, pressing harder than ever. "What superb timing, Navarro," Spectre drawled without a trace of panic in his voice.

"I said, *let her go.*"

"Is that a command, Detective? I certainly hope not. Because, considering the young woman's situation—" Spectre grabbed her by the chin and turned her face toward Sam "—offending me could prove hazardous to her health."

"I know your face. So do the ushers at the Brant Theater. You have no reason to kill her now!"

"No reason? Think again." Spectre, still holding the gun to Nina's head, nudged her forward. Toward Sam. "Move out of the way, Navarro."

"She's worthless to you—"

"But not to you."

Nina caught a glimpse of Sam's face, saw his look of helpless panic. He was gripping his gun in both hands, the barrel aimed, but he didn't dare shoot. Not with her in the line of fire.

She tried to go limp, tried to slump to the ground. No good; Spectre was too strong and he had too firm a grip around her neck. He simply dragged her beside him, his arm like a vise around her throat.

"Back off!" Spectre yelled.

"You don't want her!"

"Back off or it ends here, with her brains all over the ground!"

Sam took a step back, then another. Though his gun was still raised, it was useless to him. In that instant, Nina's gaze locked with his, and she saw more than fear, more than panic in his eyes. She saw despair.

"Nina," he said. "Nina—"

It was her last glimpse of Sam before Spectre pulled her into Sam's car. He slammed the door shut and threw the car in Reverse. Suddenly they were screeching backward down the ramp. She caught a fast-moving view of parked cars and concrete pillars, and then they crashed through the arm of the security gate.

Spectre spun the car around to face forward and hit the accelerator. They roared out of the driveway and onto the road.

Before she could recover her wits, the gun was back at her head. She looked at him, and saw a face that was frighteningly calm. The face of a man who knows he's in complete control.

"I have nothing to lose by killing you," he said.

"Then why don't you?" she whispered.

"I have plans. Plans that happen to include you."

"What plans?"

He gave a low, amused laugh. "Let's just say they involve Detective Navarro, his Bomb Squad, and a rather large amount of dynamite. I like spectacular endings, don't you?" He smiled at her.

That's when she realized whom she was looking at. What she was looking at.

A monster.

Thirteen

Sam raced down the parking garage ramp, his legs pumping with desperate speed. He emerged from the building just in time to see his car, Spectre at the wheel, careening out of the driveway and taking off down the road.

I've lost her, he thought as the taillights winked into the night. *My God. Nina...*

He sprinted to the sidewalk and ran halfway down the block before he finally came to a stop. The taillights had vanished.

The car was gone.

He gave a shout of rage, of despair, and heard his voice echo in the darkness. Too late. He was too late.

A flash of light made him spin around. A pair of headlights had just rounded the corner. Another car was approaching—one he recognized.

"Gillis!" he shouted.

The car braked to a stop near the curb. Sam dashed to the passenger door and scrambled inside.

"Go. *Go!*" he barked.

A perplexed Gillis stared at him. "What?"

"Spectre's got Nina! Move it!"

Gillis threw the car into gear. They screeched away from the curb. "Which way?"

"Left. Here!"

Gillis swerved around the corner.

Sam caught a glimpse of his own car, two blocks ahead, as it moved into an intersection and turned right.

"There!"

"I see it," Gillis said, and made the same turn.

Spectre must have spotted them, too. A moment later he accelerated and shot through a red light. Cars skidded to a stop in the intersection.

As Gillis steered through the maze of vehicles and pressed his pursuit, Sam picked up the car phone and called for assistance from all available patrol cars. With a little help, they could have Spectre boxed in.

For now, they just had to keep him in sight.

"This guy's a maniac," Gillis muttered.

"Don't lose her."

"He's gonna get us all killed. Look!"

Up ahead, Spectre swerved into the left lane, passed a car, and swerved back to the right just as a truck barreled down on him.

"Stay with them!" Sam ordered.

"I'm trying, I'm trying," Gillis, too, swerved left to pass. Too much traffic was heading toward them; he swerved back.

Seconds were lost. Seconds that Spectre pushed to his advantage.

Gillis tried again, this time managing to scoot back into his lane before colliding head-on with an oncoming van.

Spectre was nowhere in sight.

"What the hell?" muttered Gillis.

They stared at the road, saw stray taillights here and there, but otherwise it was an empty street. They drove on, through intersection after intersection, scanning the side roads. With every block they passed, Sam's panic swelled.

A half mile later, he was forced to accept the obvious. They had lost Spectre.

He had lost Nina.

Gillis was driving in grim silence now. Sam's despair had rubbed off on him as well. Neither one said it, but both of them knew. Nina was as good as dead.

"I'm sorry, Sam," murmured Gillis. "God, I'm sorry."

Sam could only stare ahead, wordless, his view blurring in a haze of tears. Moments passed. An eternity.

Patrol cars reported in. No trace of the car. Or Spectre.

Finally, at midnight, Gillis pulled over and parked at the curb. Both men sat in silence.

Gillis said, "There's still a chance."

Sam dropped his head in his hands. *A chance.* Spectre could be fifty miles away by now. Or he could be right around the corner. *What I would give for one, small chance....*

His gaze fell and he focused on Gillis's car phone.

One small chance.

He picked up the phone and dialed.

"Who're you calling?" asked Gillis.

"Spectre."

"What?"

"I'm calling my car phone." He listened as it rang. Five, six times.

Spectre answered, his voice raised in a bizarre falsetto. "Hello, you have reached the Portland Bomb Squad. No one's available to answer your call, as we seem to have misplaced our damn telephone."

"This is Navarro," growled Sam.

"Why hello, Detective Navarro. How *are* you?"

"Is she all right?"

"Who?"

"Is she all right?"

"Ah, you must be referring to the young lady. Perhaps I'll let her speak for herself."

There was a pause. He heard muffled voices, some sort of scraping sound. A soft, distant whine. Then Nina's voice came on, quiet, frightened. "Sam?"

"Are you hurt?"

"No. No, I'm fine."

"Where are you? Where's he taken you?"

"Oops," cut in Spectre. "Forbidden topic, Detective. Afraid I must abort this phone call."

"Wait. *Wait!*" cried Sam.

"Any parting words?"

"If you hurt her, Spectre—if anything happens to her— I swear I'll kill you."

"Is this a *law* enforcement officer I'm speaking to?"

"I mean it. I'll *kill* you."

"I'm shocked. *Shocked,* I tell you."

"Spectre!"

He was answered by laughter, soft and mocking. And then, abruptly, the line went dead.

Frantically Sam redialed and got a busy signal. He hung up, counted to ten, and dialed once more.

Another busy signal. Spectre had taken the phone off the hook.

Sam slammed the receiver down. "She's still alive."

"Where are they?"

"She never got the chance to tell me."

"It's been an hour. They could be anywhere within a fifty-mile radius."

"I know, I know." Sam sat back, trying to think through his swirl of panic. During his years as a cop, he'd always managed to keep his head cool, his thoughts focused. But tonight, for the first time in his career, he felt paralyzed by fear. By the knowledge that, with every moment that passed, every moment he did nothing, Nina's chances for survival faded.

"Why hasn't he killed her?" murmured Gillis. "Why is she still alive?"

Sam looked at his partner. At least Gillis still had a functioning brain. And he was thinking. Puzzling over a question that should've been obvious to them both.

"He's keeping her alive for a reason," said Gillis.

"A trump card. Insurance in case he's trapped."

"No, he's already home free. Right now, she's more of a liability than a help. Hostages slow you down. Complicate things. But he's allowed her to live."

So far, thought Sam with a wave of helpless rage. *I'm losing it, losing my ability to think straight. Her life depends on me. I can't afford to blow it.*

He looked at the phone again, and a memory echoed in his head. Something he'd heard over the phone during that brief pause between hearing Spectre's voice and Nina's. That distant wail, rising and falling.

A siren.

He reached for the phone again and dialed 911.

"Emergency operator," answered a voice.

"This is Detective Sam Navarro, Portland Police. I need

a list of all emergency dispatches made in the last twenty minutes. Anywhere in the Portland-South Portland area."

"Which vehicles, sir?"

"Everything. Ambulance, fire, police. All of them."

There was a brief silence, then another voice came on the line. Sam had his notepad ready.

"This is the supervisor, Detective Navarro," a woman said. "I've checked with the South Portland dispatcher. Combined, we've had three dispatches in the last twenty minutes. At 11:55, an ambulance was sent to 2203 Green Street in Portland. At 12:10, the police were dispatched to a burglar alarm at 751 Bickford Street in South Portland. And at 12:13, a squad car was called to the vicinity of Munjoy Hill for a report of some disturbance of the peace. There were no fire trucks dispatched during that period."

"Okay, thanks." Sam hung up and rifled through the glove compartment for a map. Quickly he circled the three dispatch locations.

"What now?" asked Gillis.

"I heard a siren over the phone, when I was talking to Spectre. Which means he had to be within hearing distance of some emergency vehicle. And these are the only three locations vehicles were dispatched to."

Gillis glanced at the map and shook his head. "We've got dozens of city blocks covered there! From point of dispatch to destination."

"But these are starting points."

"Like a haystack's a starting point."

"It's all we have to go on. Let's start at Munjoy Hill."

"This is crazy. The APB's out on your car. We've got people looking for it already. We'd be running ourselves ragged trying to chase sirens."

"Munjoy Hill, Gillis. Go."

"You're beat. I'm beat. We should go back to HQ and wait for things to develop."

"You want me to drive? Then move the hell over."

"Sam, are you *hearing* me?"

"Yes, damn you!" Sam shouted back in a sudden outburst of rage. Then, with a groan, he dropped his head in his hands. Quietly he said, "It's my fault. My fault she's going to die. They were right there in front of me. And I couldn't think of any way to save her. Any way to keep her alive."

Gillis gave a sigh of comprehension. "She means that much to you?"

"And Spectre knows it. Somehow he knows it. That's why he's keeping her alive. To torment me. Manipulate me. He has the winning hand and he's using it." He looked at Gillis. "We have to find her."

"Right now, he has the advantage. He has someone who means a lot to you. And *you're* the cop he seems to be focused on. The cop he wants to get back at." He glanced down at his car phone. It was ringing.

He answered it. "Gillis here." A moment later he hung up and started the car. "Jackman Avenue," he said, pulling into the road. "It could be our break."

"What's on Jackman Avenue?"

"An apartment, unit 338-D. They just found a body there."

Sam went very still. A sense of dread had clamped down on his chest, making it difficult to breathe. He asked, softly, "Whose body?"

"Marilyn Dukoff's."

HE WAS SINGING "Dixie!" as he worked, stringing out wire in multicolored lengths along the floor. Nina, hands and feet bound to a heavy chair, could only sit and watch help-lessly. Next to Spectre was a toolbox, a soldering iron, and two dozen dynamite sticks.

"In Dixieland where I was born, early on a frosty morn-in'…"

Spectre finished laying out the wire and turned his at-tention to the dynamite. With green electrical tape, he neatly bundled the sticks together in groups of three and set the bundles in a cardboard box.

"In Dixieland we'll make our stand, to live and die in Dixie. Away, away, away down south, in DIXIE!" he boomed out, and his voice echoed in the far reaches of the vast and empty warehouse. Then, turning to Nina, he dipped his head in a bow.

"You're crazy," whispered Nina.

"But what is madness? Who's to say?" Spectre wound green tape around the last three dynamite sticks. Then he gazed at the bundles, admiring his work. "What's that saying? 'Don't get mad, get even'? Well, I'm not mad, in any sense of the word. But I *am* going to get even."

He picked up the box of dynamite and was carrying it toward Nina when he seemed to stumble. Nina's heart almost stopped as the box of explosives tilted toward the floor. Toward her.

Spectre gave a loud gasp of horror just before he caught the box. To Nina's astonishment, he suddenly burst out laughing. "Just an old joke," he admitted. "But it never fails to get a reaction."

He really was crazy, she thought, her heart thudding.

Carrying the box of dynamite, he moved about the warehouse, laying bundles of explosives at measured inter-vals around the perimeter. "It's a shame, really," he said, "to waste so much quality dynamite on one building. But I do want to leave a good impression. A lasting impression. And I've had quite enough of Sam Navarro and his nine lives. This should take care of any extra lives he still has."

"You're laying a trap."

"You're so clever."

"Why? Why do you want to kill him?"

"Because."

"He's just a policeman doing his job."

"*Just* a policeman?" Spectre turned to her, but his expression remained hidden in the shadows of the warehouse. "Navarro is more than that. He's a challenge. My nemesis. To think, after all these years of success in cities like Boston and Miami, I should find my match in a small town like this. Not even Portland, Oregon, but Portland, *Maine.*" He gave a laugh of self-disgust. "It ends here, in this warehouse. Between Navarro and me."

Spectre crossed toward her, carrying the final bundle of dynamite. He knelt beside the rocking chair where Nina sat with hands and ankles bound. "I saved the last blast for you, Miss Cormier," he said. And he taped the bundle under Nina's chair. "You won't feel a thing," he assured her. "It will happen so fast, why, the next thing you know, you'll be sprouting angel's wings. So will Navarro. If he gets his wings at all."

"He's not stupid. He'll know you've set a trap."

Spectre began stringing out more color-coded wire now, yards and yards of it. "Yes, it should be quite obvious this isn't any run-of-the-mill bomb. All this wire, tangled up to confuse him. Circuitry that makes no sense..." He snipped a white wire, then a red one. With his soldering iron, he connected the ends. "And the time ticking away.

Minutes, then seconds. Which is the detonator wire? Which wire should he cut? The wrong one, and it all goes up in smoke. The warehouse. You. And him—if he has nerve enough to see it to the end. It's a hopeless dilemma, you see. He stays to disarm it and you could both die. He chickens out and runs, and *you* die, leaving him with guilt he'll never forget. Either way, Sam Navarro suffers. And I win."

"You can't win."

"Spare me the moralistic warnings. I have work to do. And not much time to do it." He strung the wires out to the other dynamite bundles, crisscrossing colors, splicing ends to blasting caps.

Not much time to do it, he had said. How much time was he talking about?

She glanced down at the other items laid out on the floor. A digital timer. A radio transmitter. It was to be a timed device, she realized, the countdown triggered by that transmitter. Spectre would be safely out of the building when he armed the bomb. Out of harm's way when it exploded.

Stay away, Sam, she thought. *Please stay away. And live.*

Spectre rose to his feet and glanced at his watch. "Another hour and I should be ready to make the call." He looked at her and smiled. "Three in the morning, Miss Cormier. That seems as good an hour as any to die, don't you think?"

THE WOMAN WAS NUDE from the waist down, her body crumpled on the wood floor. She had been shot once, in the head.

"The report came in at 10:45," said Yeats from Homicide. "Tenant below us noticed bloodstains seeping across the ceiling and called the landlady. She opened the door, saw the body and called us. We found the victim's ID in her purse. That's why we called you."

"Any witnesses? Anyone see anything, hear anything?" asked Gillis.

"No. He must've used a silencer. Then slipped out without being seen."

Sam gazed around at the sparsely furnished room. The walls were bare, the closets half empty, and there were boxes of clothes on the floor—all signs that Marilyn Dukoff had not yet settled into this apartment.

Yeats confirmed it. "She moved in a day ago, under the name Marilyn Brown. Paid the deposit and first month's rent in cash. That's all the landlady could tell me."

"She have any visitors?" asked Gillis.

"Next-door tenant heard a man's voice in here yesterday. But never saw him."

"Spectre," said Sam. He focused once again on the body. The criminalists were already combing the room, dusting for prints, searching for evidence. They would find none, Sam already knew; Spectre would've seen to it.

There was no point hanging around here; they'd be better off trying to chase sirens. He turned to the door, then paused as he heard one of the detectives say, "Not much in the purse. Wallet, keys, a few bills—"

"What bills?" asked Sam.

"Electric, phone. Water. Look like they're to the old apartment. The name Dukoff's on them. Delivered to a PO box."

"Let me see the phone bill."

At his first glance at the bill, Sam almost uttered a groan

of frustration. It was two sheets long and covered with long distance calls, most of them to Bangor numbers, a few to Massachusetts and Florida. It would take hours to track all those numbers down, and the chances were it would simply lead them to Marilyn Dukoff's bewildered friends or family.

Then he focused on one number, at the bottom of the bill. It was a collect call charge, from a South Portland prefix, dated a week and a half ago at 10:17 p.m. Someone had called collect and Marilyn Dukoff had accepted the charges.

"This could be something," Sam noted. "I need the location of this number."

"We can call the operator from my car," said Gillis. "but I don't know what it's going to get you."

"A hunch. That's what I'm going on," Sam admitted.

Back in Gillis's car, Sam called the Directory Assistance supervisor.

After checking her computer, she confirmed it was a pay phone. "It's near the corner of Calderwood and Hardwick, in South Portland."

"Isn't there a gas station on that corner?" asked Sam. "I seem to remember one there."

"There may be, Detective. I can't tell you for certain."

Sam hung up and reached for the South Portland map. Under the dome light, he pinpointed the location of the pay phone. "Here it is," he said to Gillis.

"There's just some industrial buildings out there."

"Yeah, which makes a collect call at 10:17 p.m. all the more interesting."

"Could've been anyone calling her. Friends, family. For all we know—"

"It was Spectre," Sam said. His head jerked up in sudden excitement. "South Portland. Let's *go*."

"What?"

Sam thrust the map toward Gillis. "Here's Bickford Street. A squad car was dispatched there at 12:10. And here's Calderwood and Hardwick. The squad car would've gone right through this area."

"You think Spectre's holed up around there?"

Sam scrawled a circle on the map, a three-block radius around Calderwood and Hardwick. "He's here. He's got to be around here."

Gillis started the car. "I think our haystack just got a hell of a lot smaller."

Twenty minutes later, they were at the corner of Hardwick and Calderwood. There was, indeed, a gas station there, but it had been closed down and a For Sale—Commercial Property sign was posted in the scraggly strip of a garden near the road. Sam and Gillis sat in their idling car for a moment, scanning the street. There was no other traffic in sight.

Gillis began to drive up Hardwick. The neighborhood was mostly industrial. Vacant lots, a boating supply outlet. A lumber wholesaler. A furniture maker. Everything was closed for the night, the parking lots empty, the buildings dark. They turned onto Calderwood.

A few hundred yards later, Sam spotted the light. It was faint, no more than a yellowish glow from a small window—the only window in the building. As they pulled closer, Gillis cut his headlights. They stopped half a block away.

"It's the old Stimson warehouse," said Sam.

"No cars in the lot," Gillis noted. "But it looks like someone's home."

"Didn't the Stimson cannery close down last year?"

Sam didn't answer; he was already stepping out of the car.

"Hey!" whispered Gillis. "Shouldn't we call for backup?"

"You call. I'm checking it out."

"Sam!" Gillis hissed. "Sam!"

Adrenaline pumping, Sam ignored his partner's warnings and started toward the warehouse. The darkness was in his favor; whoever was inside wouldn't be able to spot his approach. Through the cracks in the truck bay doors, he saw more light, vertical slivers of yellow.

He circled the building, but spotted no ground floor windows, no way to look inside. There was a back door and a front door, but both were locked.

At the front of the building, he met up with Gillis.

"Backup's on the way," Gillis informed him.

"I have to get in there."

"We don't know what we'll find in there—" Gillis suddenly paused and glanced at his car.

The phone was ringing.

Both men scurried back to answer it.

Sam grabbed the receiver. "Navarro here."

"Detective Navarro," said the police operator. "We have an outside phone call for you. The man says it's urgent. I'll put it through."

There was a pause, a few clicks, and then a man's voice said, "I'm so glad to reach you, Detective. This car phone of yours is coming in handy."

"Spectre?"

"I'd like to issue a personal invitation, Detective. To you and you alone. A reunion, with a certain someone who's right here beside me."

"Is she all right?"

"She's perfectly fine." Spectre paused and added with a soft tone of threat. "For the moment."

"What do you want from me?"

"Nothing at all. I'd just like you to come and take Miss Cormier off my hands. She's becoming an inconvenience. And I have other places to go to."

"Where is she?"

"I'll give you a clue. Herring."

"What?"

"Maybe the name *Stimson* rings a bell? You can look up the address. Sorry I won't be here to greet you, but I really *must* be going."

SPECTRE HUNG UP the phone and smiled at Nina. "Time for me to go. Lover boy should be here any minute." He picked up his toolbox and set it in the car, which he'd driven through the loading bay to keep it out of sight.

He's leaving, she thought. *Leaving me as bait for the trap.*

It was cool in the warehouse, but she felt a drop of sweat slide down her temple as she watched Spectre reach down for the radio transmitter. All he had to do was flick one switch on that radio device, and the bomb would be armed, the countdown started.

Ten minutes later, it would explode.

Her heart gave a painful thud as she saw him reach for the radio switch. Then he smiled at her.

"Not yet," he said. "I wouldn't want things to happen prematurely."

Turning, he walked toward the truck bay door. He gave Nina a farewell salute. "Say goodbye to Navarro for me. Tell him I'm so sorry to miss the big kaboom." He unlatched the bay door and gave the handle a yank. It slid up with the sound of grating metal. It was almost open when Spectre suddenly froze.

Right in front of him, a pair of headlights came on.

"Freeze, Spectre!" came a command from somewhere in the darkness. "Hands over your head!"

Sam, thought Nina. *You found me....*

"Hands up!" yelled Sam. "Do it!"

Silhouetted against the headlights, Spectre seemed to hesitate for a few seconds. Then, slowly, he raised his hands over his head.

He was still holding the transmitter.

"Sam!" cried Nina. "There's a bomb! He's got a transmitter!"

"Put it down," Sam ordered. "Put it down or I shoot!"

"Certainly," agreed Spectre. Slowly he dropped to a crouch and lowered the transmitter toward the floor. But as he lay it down, there was a distinct *click* that echoed through the warehouse.

My God, he's armed the bomb, thought Nina.

"Better run," said Spectre. And he dived sideways, toward a stack of crates.

He wasn't fast enough. In the next instant, Sam squeezed off two shots. Both bullets found their target.

Spectre seemed to stumble. He dropped to his knees and began to crawl forward, but his limbs were moving drunkenly, like a swimmer trying to paddle across land. He was making gurgling sounds now, gasping out curses with his last few breaths.

"Dead," wheezed Spectre, and it was almost a laugh. "You're all dead...."

Sam stepped over Spectre's motionless body and started straight toward Nina.

"No!" she cried. "Stay away!"

He stopped dead, staring at her with a look of bewilderment. "What is it?"

"He's wired a bomb to my chair," sobbed Nina. "If you try to cut me loose it'll go off!"

At once Sam's gaze shot to the coils of wire ringing her chair, then followed the trail of wire to the warehouse wall, to the first bundle of dynamite, lying in plain view.

"He has eighteen sticks planted all around the building," she said. "Three are under my chair. It's set to go off in ten minutes. Less, now."

Their gazes met. And in that one glance she saw his look of panic. It was quickly suppressed. He stepped across the wire and crouched by her chair.

"I'm getting you out of here," he vowed.

"There's not enough time!"

"Ten minutes?" He gave a terse laugh. "That's loads of time." He knelt down and peered under the seat. He didn't say a thing, but when he rose again, his expression was grim. He turned and called, "Gillis?"

"Right here," Gillis answered, stepping gingerly over the wires. "I got the toolbox. What do we have?"

"Three sticks under the chair, and a digital timer." Sam gently slid out the timing device, bristling with wires, and set it carefully on the floor. "It looks like a simple series-parallel circuit. I'll need time to analyze it."

"How long do we have?"

"Eight minutes and forty-five seconds and counting."

Gillis cursed. "No time to get the bomb truck."

A wail of a siren suddenly cut through the night. Two police cruisers pulled up outside the bay door.

"Backup's here," Gillis said. He hurried over to the doors, waving at the other cops. "Stay back!" he yelled. "We got a bomb in here! I want a perimeter evac *now!* And get an ambulance here on standby."

I won't need an ambulance, thought Nina. *If this bomb goes off, there'll be nothing left of me to pick up.*

She tried to calm her racing heart, tried to stop her slide toward hysteria, but sheer terror was making it hard for her to breathe. There was nothing she could do to save herself. Her wrists were tightly bound; so were her ankles. If she so much as shifted too far in her chair, the bomb could be triggered.

It was all up to Sam.

Fourteen

Sam's jaw was taut as he studied the tangle of wires and circuitry. There were so many wires! It would take an hour just to sort them all out. But all they had were minutes. Though he didn't say a word, she could read the urgency in his face, could see the first droplets of sweat forming on his forehead.

Gillis returned to his partner's side. "I checked the perimeter. Spectre's got the building wired with fifteen or more sticks. No other action fuses as far as I can see. The brain to this whole device is right there in your hands."

"It's too easy," muttered Sam, scanning the circuitry. "He *wants* me to cut this wire."

"Could it be a double feint? He knew we'd be suspicious. So he made it simple on purpose—just to throw us?"

Sam swallowed. "This looks like the arming switch right here. But over here, he's got the cover soldered shut. He could have a completely different switch inside. Magnetic reed or a Castle-Robins device. If I pry off that cap, it could fire."

Gillis glanced at the digital timer. "Five minutes left."

"I know, I know." Sam's voice was hoarse with tension, but his hands were absolutely steady as he traced the circuitry. One tug on the wrong wire, and all three of them could be instantly vaporized.

Outside, more sirens whined to a stop. Nina could hear voices, the sounds of confusion.

But inside, there was silence.

Sam took a breath and glanced up at her. "You okay?"

She gave a tense nod. And she saw, in his face, the first glimpse of panic. *He won't figure this out in time, and he knows it.*

This was just what Spectre had planned. The hopeless dilemma. The fatal choice. Which wire to cut? One? None? Does he gamble with his own life? Or does he make the rational choice to abandon the building—and her?

She knew the choice he would make. She could see it in his eyes.

They were both going to die.

"Two and a half minutes," said Gillis.

"Go on, get out of here," Sam ordered.

"You need an extra pair of hands."

"And your kids need a father. Get the hell out."

Gillis didn't budge.

Sam picked up the wire cutters and isolated a white wire.

"You're guessing, Sam. You don't know."

"Instinct, buddy. I've always had good instincts. Better leave. We're down to two minutes. And you're not doing me any good."

Gillis rose to his feet, but lingered there, torn between leaving and staying. "Sam—"

"Move."

Gillis said, softly, "I'll have a bottle of Scotch waiting for you, buddy."

"You do that. Now get out of here."

Without another word, Gillis left the building.

Only Sam and Nina remained. *He doesn't have to stay,* she thought. *He doesn't have to die.*

"Sam," she whispered.

He didn't seem to hear her; he was concentrating too hard on the circuit board, his wire cutters hovering between a life-and-death choice.

"Leave, Sam," she begged.

"This is my job, Nina."

"It's not your job to die!"

"We're not going to die."

"You're right. *We* aren't. *You* aren't. If you leave now—"

"I'm not leaving. You understand? I'm *not.*" His gaze rose to meet hers. And she saw, in those steady eyes, that he had made up his mind. He'd made the choice to live— or die—with her. This was not the cop looking at her, but the man who loved her. The man *she* loved.

She felt tears trickle down her face. Only then did she realize she was crying.

"We're down to a minute. I'm going to make a guess here," he said. "If I'm right, cutting this wire should do the trick. If I'm wrong…" He let out a breath. "We'll know pretty quick one way or the other." He slipped the teeth of the cutter around the white wire. "Okay, I'm going with this one."

"Wait."

"What is it?"

"When Spectre was putting it together, he soldered a white wire to a red one, then he covered it all up with green tape. Does that make a difference?"

Sam stared down at the wire he'd been about to cut. "It does," he said softly. "It makes a hell of a lot of difference."

"Sam!" came Gillis's shout through a megaphone. "You've got ten seconds left!"

Ten seconds to run.

Sam didn't run. He moved the wire cutter to a black wire and positioned the jaws to cut. Then he stopped and looked up at Nina.

They stared at each other one last time.

"I love you," he said.

She nodded, the tears streaming down her face. "I love you too," she whispered.

Their gazes remained locked, unwavering, as he slowly closed the cutter over the wire. Even as the jaws came together, even as the teeth bit into the plastic coating, Sam was looking at her, and she at him.

The wire snapped in two.

For a moment neither one of them moved. They were still frozen in place, still paralyzed by the certainty of death.

Then, outside, Gillis yelled, "Sam? You're past countdown! *Sam!*"

All at once, Sam was cutting the bonds from her hands, her ankles. She was too numb to stand, but she didn't need to. He gathered her up into his arms and carried her out of the warehouse, into the night.

Outside, the street was ablaze with the flashing lights of emergency vehicles: squad cars, ambulances, fire trucks. Sam carried her safely past the yellow police tape and set her down on her feet.

Instantly they were surrounded by a mob of officials, Chief Coopersmith and Liddell among them, all clamoring to know the bomb's status. Sam ignored them all. He just stood there with his arms around Nina, shielding her from the chaos.

"Everyone back!" shouted Gillis, waving the crowd away. "Give 'em some breathing space!" He turned to Sam. "What about the device?"

"It's disarmed," said Sam. "But be careful. Spectre may have left us one last surprise."

"I'll take care of it." Gillis started toward the warehouse, then turned back. "Hey, Sam?"

"Yeah?"

"I'd say you just earned your retirement." Gillis grinned. And then he walked away.

Nina looked up at Sam. Though the danger was over, she could still feel his heart pounding, could feel her own heart beating just as wildly.

"You didn't leave me," she whispered, new tears sliding down her face. "You could have—"

"No, I couldn't."

"I told you to go! I *wanted* you to go."

"And I wanted to stay." He took her face in his hands. Firmly, insistently. "There was no other place I'd be but right there beside you, Nina. There's no other place I ever want to be."

She knew a dozen pairs of eyes were watching them. Already the news media had arrived with their camera flashbulbs and their shouted questions. The night was alive with voices and multicolored lights. But at that moment, as he held her, as they kissed, there was no one else but Sam.

When dawn broke, he would still be holding her.

Epilogue

The wedding was on. No doubt about it.

Accompanied by a lilting Irish melody played by flute and harp, Nina and her father walked arm in arm into the forest glade. There, beneath the fiery brilliance of autumn foliage, stood Sam. Just as she knew he would be.

He was grinning, as nervous as a rookie cop on his first beat. Beside him stood his best man, Gillis, and Reverend Sullivan, both wearing smiles. A small circle of friends and family stood gathered under the trees: Wendy and her husband. Chief Coopersmith. Nina's colleagues from the hospital. Also among the guests was Lydia, looking quietly resigned to the fact her daughter was marrying a mere cop.

Some things in life, thought Nina, cannot be changed. She had accepted that. Perhaps Lydia, some day, would learn to be as accepting.

The music faded, and the leaves of autumn drifted down in a soft rain of red and orange. Sam reached out to her. His smile told her all she needed to know. This was right; this was meant to be.

She took his hand.